Volume 2

Airship 27 Productions

The Adventures of Radio Rita Volume 2

An Airship 27 Production
www.airship27.com
www.airship27hangar.com

Editor: Ron Fortier
Associate Editor: Myles Robertson
Production Designer: Rob Davis
Marketing and promotion: Michael Vance

ISBN: 978-1-969285-10-3

Printed in the United States of America

10 9 8 7 6 5 4 3 2 1

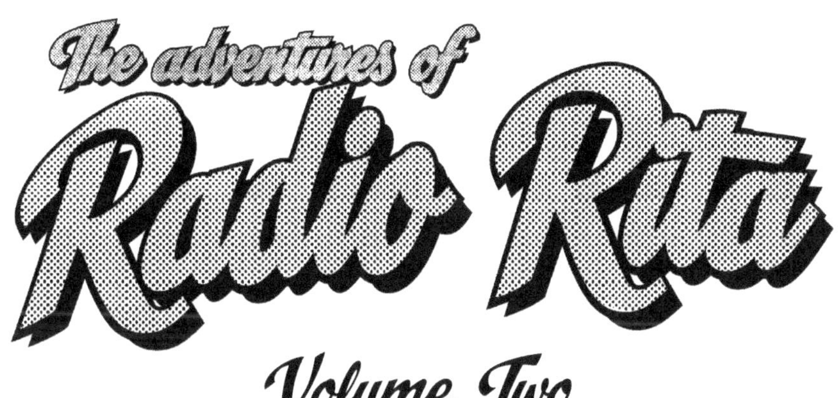

Volume Two
Contents

The Great Race

by Curtis Fernlund

Roosevelt Field
Mineola Township
Long Island, New York
1935

"Wa-HOOooo!"

Rita whooped as the old Bellanca CH-400 banked sharply to the right. The ground far below slipped away as Long Island Sound and the Atlantic beyond filled the windscreen before her. She pulled back on the control-stick between her long legs and jiggled the throttle-lever, urging the rebuilt Skyrocket to climb.

"Gahhh…

"Rita," the mechanic for the airfield yelled from the seat behind her, his white-knuckled grip on the back of her own seat digging into the worn leather. "Don't push her so hard. She wasn't designed for tricks; she's a damn transport for Chris sake." Rita laughed.

"Relax, 'Monkey'," she said as she leveled out the plane checking the altimeter and horizon indicator. She had the utility plane holding at just over two miles; well below its ceiling of twenty thousand feet with plenty of margin for error. "It's all good," she assured as she set the Bellanca to yaw right-and-left, turning back towards the field in a sloping turn.

"Don't," Monkey Parker screamed again as the aircraft whined with the sudden torque. "Dammit; you're gonna blow the engine." Rita laughed again.

Jimmy "Monkey" Parker swore he was twenty, but Rita had her doubts. He was the youngest mechanic she ever met, though he was also the best, at least at Roosevelt Field. He was cute in his own way with long brown hair barely held in check by a filthy, New York Dodgers baseball cap, thin and lanky, though shorter than her own 5' 8" with long, gangly limbs. Despite his abilities though, Jimmy was still considered a grease-monkey, like most mechanics and always seemed to fit that bill. His coveralls were usually stained black, and no matter how hard he scrubbed, he always seemed to have a smear somewhere on his face. Add to that his skinny frame, well, the nickname "Monkey" took hold one day and never let go.

"Language, James," Rita scolded, sharply pitching the plane's nose down back towards the ground. "My Mama Rose always said: "Don't take the Lord's name in vain."

Rita pulled out of her descent and leveled at 1000 feet as Roosevelt Field came back into clear view, still a few miles southwest. She could see Mineola and Garden City easily now, and far to the western horizon the gray smudge of Manhattan's towering skyline beckoning. She checked her instruments again, scanning the many lighted dials and meters: the short-range radio navigation in communication with the field's beacon, true altitude and airspeed, and rate of turn. All of them looked good.

COUGH!

BANG!

Rita felt the yoke jerk in her hand as the engine sputtered and spat. A great gout of gray smoke gushed from the motor, obscuring her view for a moment until the cloud started streaming out alongside the plane to the left. Rita ground on the control, gripping it tight as it tried to pull to the right. She eased off the throttle slowing the gasoline flow to the engine, her feet off the floor panels to set the old plane to cruise.

BANG!

"I knew it! I knew it," Monkey screamed, leaning forward until his head was right next to hers. He pointed at the second stream of smoke whipping out to the right. "You've blown the plugs," he yowled in her ear, "probably burned the carburetor. God, we're gonna crash!"

"Will you get back in your seat," Rita hissed, muscling the joystick to bend to her will. The Skyrocket was beginning to slow but was shaking wildly and there was still a fog of dark smoke gushing from the rebuilt radial engine on both sides. They were probably burning oil from whatever spark caused the first sputter, and before long she knew the Pratt & Whitney Wasp engine would most likely light up. "Sit down, shut up and buckle in."

Rita pulled her bulky headphones from the hook below the control panel and slipped them over her ears. Immediately she grit her teeth at the shrill squeal of static coming through. She reached out and adjusted the radio dial to a lower frequency and heard the raspy, familiar voice urgently calling:

"Skyrocket 303NC, this is Roosevelt… Status and ears on."

Once the static and squawk cleared she adjusted the gain on the radio and responded:

"Roosevelt, this is Skyrocket 303NC at four-point-eight miles out east and in," she glanced at Monkey in the small, circular mirror she had dangling from the side-panel, "slight distress. Requesting a clear approach, please, Steve."

"Skyrocket 303NC; is that you Rita? Over."

"Roger, Roosevelt. Over."

"Skyrocket 303NC; I might have known," STATIC, "Switch frequency to

118.50 and hold steady for approach at 500. Note Traffic at two o'clock high, three miles at LZ 127 at 758."

COUGH!

"Dammit!"

Rita eased on the throttle a bit as she looked up, forward and to the right as something caught her eye. She stared in wonder at the huge airship, the *Graf Zeppelin* floating lazily towards the northwest some three miles distant. The German zeppelin was truly a sight to behold.

"Rita," Monkey shouted, breaking her momentary awe as she heard the radio screeching again. She adjusted the gain as the last message repeated:

"Skyrocket 303NC; LZ 127 en route to Lakehurst, moving away and out of path at 38 knots. All other traffic clear to Brooklyn, Bennet."

"Roger, Roosevelt. Skyrocket 303NC holding at 500 at two miles. Still approaching Roosevelt from northeast; Requests the active."

BANG!

"Oh god; we're all gonna die."

"Jeez, Monkey," Rita said covering the microphone, "a little faith, huh?" Rita turned her attention back to Roosevelt Field's, Air-Traffic Control, such as it was.

"Skyrocket 303NC; active is at Roosevelt three two. Request status."

"Roosevelt; Skyrocket 303NC with minor engine trouble. Roosevelt traffic, Skyrocket 303NC is one mile to the east, to enter the left downwind for runway three two, Roosevelt."

"Skyrocket 303NC; A-firmative. Hold course and beacon. Reduce speed and descent at markers."

"Roger, Roosevelt."

"Skyrocket 303NC; request fire services?"

"Roosevelt; negative. Burning oil; no fire evident, Roosevelt."

"Roger, Skyrocket 303NC. Hold steady and reduce airspeed at marker three."

"Wilco, Roosevelt.

Rita continued to pull back on the joystick slightly, easing the Bellanca's nose up as she tapped on the foot pedals to slow her speed and help with the slight turbulence she felt in the opposing winds blowing in off the Sound. The zeppelin was far off and behind her, thank God. She didn't want some midair disaster with a big bag of hydrogen. Despite the winds, the weather was clear as far as she could see save for the usual smog perpetually hanging about Manhattan, the ceiling at 18,000 feet at last report, not a low cloud in the sky.

"Skyrocket 303NC, stay on heading. Looking good. Fire standing by, Rita; over."

"Roosevelt; thanks Steve. On heading one-eight-zero and descending. No issues."

BOOM!

"Jesus, what—," Monkey shrieked as something flew off the fuselage and his fingers suddenly dug into her shoulders. Rita winced in pain, trying to shake him off, losing sight of the field barely a quarter mile away. "What was that?"

"I dunno," Rita shouted pushing forward on the joystick and almost sending the plane into a nosedive. The old Bellanca rattled and shook at the sudden strain, the noise of the faltering engine growing in pitch. "Let go!"

Monkey did, easing back in his seat as Rita fought to control the plane. She cut the throttle to almost nil and eased back on the control-stick again, watching her horizon and altimeter as she came closer to her landing. Gray smoke billowed over the windscreen and spats of oil smeared against the glass in blotches, obscuring her vision even more. The Wasp was gasping for breath as she flicked switches and spun the dials to get the airspeed down, struggling to keep the bucking plane level. She threw US Civil regulations out the window as she called the field.

"I've got problems, Steve," she shouted into the mike, "I can't see the field. Repeat: I'm flying blind."

"God—"

"Just hold steady, Rita," Stephen Finch shouted back, concern in his voice, "you're dead on target. Slow and steady wins the race."

"Got'cha," Rita replied as she dipped the Bellanca down again trying to clear the flowing smoke. She saw the occasional spark flaring from the Wasp motor as she wobbled the wings, hoping to clear her immediate vision. Suddenly Roosevelt Field was right below her.

She threw herself back into her seat, her foot slamming on the brake as she jerked the stick deep within her legs. The plane lurched violently; screaming as the nose rose abruptly, blotting out the runway.

"More, Rita," Steve's staticky voice shouted in her ears. She was practically standing with her back pressed into her seat, grinding on the joystick. She grit her teeth as the runway loomed.

"More, dammit!"

She cut the engine and pulled back with all her weight and strength to get the nose up high as Monkey squealed in a panic. She heard the screech as the plane heaved then lurched, touching down on the tarmac before bouncing back up. The Skyrocket tilted left-and-right as it struggled in flight; spastic jumps bouncing down the runway. She knew the asphalt ran some 2000 feet, and she sensed she was about halfway down its length trying to slow the plane.

The Bellanca bounced.

Then bounced again…

There was forest ahead and the township of Mineola beyond that. She did not want to crash into the woods so, in desperation, bore the stick to the right, out onto the surrounding sod and grass. She continued to lean, forcing the Skyrocket into a tight turn as it bucked and bounced over the grounds surrounding the airport. Finally the old plane listed briefly to the right and settled, coming to a halt. Rita let out a breath she didn't realize she was holding. She heard poor Jimmy retching in the seat behind her.

"Are we down?" he gasped and Rita smiled as the radio crackled again.

"Are you okay, Rita?" Steve shouted on his end. The reverb squealed in her ears.

"Yeah," she answered to both men, settling back into her seat with a sigh, high on adrenaline. She heard sirens approaching and saw Roosevelt's lone firetruck pealing towards her, an ambulance close behind. She had no idea where that came from—probably Mineola called in by Steve, bless him—but she was happy to see it. Monkey probably needed it more than her. "Yeah, we're both fine."

"Glad to hear," he said followed by a long pause. "Well, not a perfect 3-pointer, but ya' did good."

"Thanks," she replied and glanced back at Jimmy still doubled-over with his head between his legs. "Any landing you can walk away from, right?"

Steve laughed as the engine finally burst into flames.

"Here comes Mister Lebreque."

Rita turned her attention from the firemen still hosing down the smoldering Bianca and looked towards the hangars. She was standing near Parker, rubbing his shoulder as he sat on the back bumper of the Mineola ambulance Steve called in, gulping and breathing into a small paper bag—hyperventilating Captain Spalding of the Roosevelt Field Reserves told her. He also said the engine simply had a grease fire; excess grease burning on the refurbished Wasp motor and not as bad as it seemed. That was good.

She saw the burly, black man running towards the scene and not looking happy as he stared at his downed airplane. Lebreque was over six-feet tall with dark skin rippling with muscles as he ran. He was handsome and well-built, at least in her opinion. He was a man of many talents too: intelligent, well-spoken in at least five languages, a licensed pilot, weapons expert from his twenty-year stint in the US Army Special Forces, and a martial arts expert she had heard. Rita was impressed, but if that wasn't enough, the man was an acclaimed chef in Manhattan, at Delmonico's no less; one of the ritziest restaurants in the city; at least when he was not cooking up mouth-watering dishes right here on the field for Hangar 27.

"He'll be fine in a few minutes," the ambulance attendant assured her as she patted Monkey's back, "just a little air-sickness I think. I gave him some bromo-seltzer to settle his stomach."

"Thanks," Rita told the man as she went to face Lebreque. She forced a smile and casual attitude as though nothing had happened.

"Hello, Pierre."

"I hope you didn't break my plane, Rita." She could hear her friend's French accent from growing up in New Orleans and a time in France at the Sorbonne School of Culinary Arts, where he developed his cooking expertise. She could also hear his concern as he stared at his still-smoldering transport.

"*Moi*," she asked innocently. Rita flashed her best smile trying to look coy. Lebreque closed his eyes and rubbed a hand over his face. She could see he was trying to remain calm.

"What the…heck happened," he asked after a deep breath." He turned between her, Stephen Finch and the plane. The firemen seemed to be finished and were gathering their gear back onto their old pumper. Rita shrugged.

"Monkey said I was gonna blow the engine; pushing it too hard with a few harmless aerobatics. I don't think it's that bad; just blew a couple spark plugs probably, and that started the fire, looks worse than it was."

"It looks pretty damn bad, Rita."

"Hey, we had to get the Gremlins out, right? Better I do it now than in the middle of a charter."

Chef Pierre, grimaced then nodded, accepting that. Rita knew he wanted to start up a charter flight service ferrying five or six passengers in his Skyrocket from Roosevelt into Floyd Bennet Field and Flushing Airport closer to Manhattan. A great idea, as the Long Island Railroad trip could take hours at times and the Long Island Motor Parkway could become jammed with traffic. He'd make a fortune if he could get his endeavor off the ground, so to speak. He sighed.

"You're right," he admitted as he unclenched his fists and relaxed a little. "You're always right. I'm glad you weren't hurt."

"Thanks." Rita smiled as he jogged off towards the plane, the firemen signaling all was clear. He'd be okay after he assessed the damage.

"Damn good landing, Rita," Steve Finch finally spoke up, "all things considered."

"Thanks to you, pal." They shared a smile then both heard the sputtering sounds of an approaching plane. Rita shielded her eyes against the sunlight and saw a Grumman XSBF Biplane circling the field awaiting clearance.

"Duty calls," Finch said giving her a quick salute before trotting off towards the hangars. She heard the firetruck rev to life and pull away, soon followed by the ambulance, heading back to the township, leaving Monkey standing beside her still holding his bag. He looked pale and drained.

"Guess I better call Tiny to bring out his tow-truck for the Bellanca," he said but Rita waved him away.

"I got it. You just go get some rest, a good night's sleep; after that, the plane. Tomorrow's another day."

Jimmy "Monkey" Parker gave her a wan smile before heading off to his mechanic's hut and garage behind the hangars. Rita watched him for a moment then sighed. With a final glance at the plane and Pierre, she headed for Hangar 27.

Union Square Park
New York City

The trip into Manhattan had been a long one as expected. Not quite thirty miles 'as the crow flies.' The ride on the Long Island Railroad took well over an hour on what they called the *Main Line*. First from Mineola to Jamaica Station, where they had to wait for their connection to the next train through the East River Tunnels to get to Pennsylvania Station, a mere fifteen minutes away. Thankfully, as Rita was getting antsy when she and Pierre finally disembarked the train onto the crowded, smoky station platform. Strange how she could cram herself into a tiny airplane cockpit for any length of time but put her in a car or train, or even on a cruise ship, and she felt she might quickly go mad.

"It's because you're not in control, *Cheri*," Chef Pierre told her one night in Hangar 27 after another mouth-watering, late-night supper he had prepared for the flight crew. She remembered Monkey was there in the background hammering on the engines of *Airship* 27—the huge signature zeppelin of the flight company—along with Captain Ron, the ship's Sky-pilot, and his right-hand-man and Chief Engineer, Commander Davis. Just a few old, dear friends sitting around one night after a great meal drinking warm brandy, cold beer, and chewing the fat.

"You want to be in control of your *le destin*— your fate. You are fine, even thrilled when faced with your own *la fin*. You crave it. But, you do not like putting your life in the hands of others."

"La *fin*?" Rita asked, swirling her brandy.

"*Death*," Captain Ron offered with a nod, "and he's right. You're a thrill-seeker, Rita. We all are, in our own way, I suppose. However, you're never going to be happy. There's always going to be one more thing to do. Another record to break, another mountain to climb."

"And we love you for it," the Commander added with a grin. "Don't get us wrong. We just—"

"Dammit!"

Everyone turned as Monkey cursed and the sound of a wrench clattering to the floor. More expletives echoed as everyone chuckled, the somber mood broken.

"We just love you, *Cheri*," Pierre cut in after a long pause. "We don't want to see you hurt."

Rita could not remember just what she finally replied—something flip no doubt—but she knew they were right. But what was wrong with loving life and the thrills it brought? She always thought they were all only here for a short time on God's Green Earth, so make the most of it.

"So, would you like to stop by the Green Market with me or not?"

"What?"

Rita looked up and around, surprised to find herself outside Pennsylvania Station on 8th Avenue; the very heart of Manhattan. She buttoned her flight jacket higher, raising the sheepskin collar against the brisk breeze blowing in off the Hudson River to the west, looking around and actually gawking as she always did whenever she visited the greatest city in the world. She could see the Empire State Building just a few avenues east, the Chrysler Building further uptown and other skyscrapers she could not name, all stretching high and magnificent. She always got a thrill to be in the city. Not only the buildings, but the crowds and non-stop, fast-paced action all the time in the 'City that Never Sleeps'. She loved it.

"What?" she repeated, and Pierre chuckled.

"The Green Market down in Union Square Park. I want to pick up some special quality ingredients for tonight's menu at Delmonico's. It won't take long."

"Sure," she answered. "Any chance to see the city."

Pierre smiled and offered his arm and the two walked the short distance west over to Seventh where her companion stepped right out into the street to hail one of the many yellow cabs maneuvering swiftly down the avenue. The hack they got was well-worn inside with tattered seats and cigarette butts on the floor, but warm. And the cabby was a wiz at dodging in-and-out of the steady throng of traffic: cars, other cabs and delivery panel vans. Rita felt that antsy-ness again, but could not find a seatbelt in the back compartment, so she held tightly to the overhead strap as the car screeched to a halt on 14th Street

" You're a thrill-seeker, Rita."

across from the park. Pierre paid the cabby and the two piled out.

"I need to see if M'boy is here today, hopefully. An' I want to see what the other stalls have to offer. I need some Southern greens and a few more-exotic peppers. It shouldn't take long."

"Mmmm… Peppers." Rita loved her spicy foods: another thrill? She had no idea and couldn't imagine what Pierre might be cooking-up for dinner tonight. Something fabulous she was sure. "Sure. I love this."

Rita was about to take his arm again but her eyes suddenly lit up as she spied a New York street-cart parked on the corner. She licked her lips and immediately headed off saying, over her shoulder, "I'll catch up."

Rita charged right up to the vender's cart, waiting impatiently while a portly woman bought a hot pretzel. She licked her lips as the woman added mustard and grabbed napkins, blocking the cart before finally moving away so she could step forward.

"What'cher fare, girlie," the grizzled old man servicing the cart asked without looking up. He sounded gruff and looked grimy in his filthy apron and soiled green fedora, a cigar butt smoldering from the corner of his lips, but she didn't care. It was all part of the show.

"Gimme a foot-long with the works," she ordered happily and pulled her shoulder-bag to dig for her wallet as the man grumbled something as he retrieved his semi-clean tongs. He pulled out a hotdog bun and opened it, adding a coating of mayonnaise on the bread. He then opened the panel where the heated water-dogs floated, plucking one out and quickly shutting the lid before placing the steamy foot-long sausage on the bun. The hot wiener hung over the edges as he slathered on mustard, catsup, relish and onions over the length of the red-hot. Rita's mouth was watering as he cradled it in a paper napkin and handed her her feast. She passed back the required dime and added in a nickel with a wide smile of appreciation.

"Thanks," they said in unison, and Rita turned away taking a huge bite and almost dying with delight. She was surely in heaven it tasted so good. There was nothing like an New York City water-dog. Nothing!

After another bite she scanned the busy market for her friend. Not too far from the subway kiosk she spotted him haggling with a vendor at a stall. She casually sauntered over taking in the sights, sounds, and especially all the luscious smells of the Green Market. There were, of course, fresh vegetables as far as the eye could see—greens and onions, tomatoes, potatoes and other tubers —all arriving fresh that morning from the farms on Long Island and the outer burroughs. She saw meats packed on ice, the morning catch of fresh fish, and breads probably from the Brooklyn bakeries. And oh, the fruits. She swore next time she was in the city she would partake, but tonight the dinner was on Chef

Pierre, and the hotdog would tide her over until then. Well, maybe a pretzel before she left.

The stall vendor was just bagging up some habanero peppers as she reached Pierre's side. He already had a huge loaf of what smelled like authentic San Francisco sourdough bread under one arm and a bag in the other sporting green onion stalks out the top. He gave the man four-bits as he turned around and first smiled at Rita, then frowned when he saw what she was eating.

"*Mon dieux*," he muttered as he looked at her face dripping relish down her chin, "how can you eat that?"

"It's delicious," she said, sliding the last couple inches of the dog into her mouth and chewing like a five-year-old; open-mouthed and enjoying every bite. He shook his head as she swallowed and licked her lips with a loud 'SMACK' before wadding up the papers and tossing them in a nearby trash receptacle. "*Nathan's* are better, but that was great. Try one before you knock it."

"Never," he groused but he had to smile at her enthusiasm. He stuffed the smaller, pepper bag into the larger and tried to fit the bread in as well but finally gave up to look around, then at her.

"I think I'm done here. Are you coming to the restaurant now, or will I see you later?"

"I want to get a shower, nap and change of clothes first. Probably grab a room for the day at the Jeanne d'Arc Boarding House over on Fifteenth." She gestured off to the west. "I've stayed there before. It's clean and quiet and I need some sleep. Then maybe explore the streets for awhile." Chef Pierre grimaced but finally shrugged.

"As you wish," he conceded. "Just let me know when you get to the restaurant. I'll have a table waiting for you and your date." He said the last word with a bit of venom and Rita laughed.

"No worries, Pierre. You'll always be number one in my heart…Or at least my stomach."

Radio Rita laughed as she strolled off into the crowd.

It wasn't far to the old Boarding House on 15th Street from Union Square, and the weather was great with blue skies, high, wispy clouds and a brisk breeze adding a definite brace to the air. Truly, on such a glorious day, Rita would just as soon forget about dinner and spend the day enjoying Manhattan; the parks, museums, the lights of Times Square at night. It was tempting, but Pierre seemed to be going to extra efforts for his meal preparations for tonight's dinner at Delmonico's, so she supposed she should attend and make her friend happy. Plus, she wanted to see Brad.

Rita smiled, thinking of her old friend as she walked down 14th Street, looking in the shop windows and perusing the vendor stalls lined up along the crosstown boulevard. There were book stores, clothing shops, restaurants and more side-by-side in the building fronts with apartments and offices in the upper floors. It wasn't far from here, in fact, she had first met Bradley Morgan, running into him—quite literally—as he came dashing out of one of the upper offices into the street and smack into her. They sprawled on the sidewalk in a frantic panic, Rita thinking the worst and Brad apologizing over and over as he helped her to her feet, blushing as he brushed her off and gathered his stray papers before they were caught by the wind. The two finally laughed over the whole incident as they walked to 6th Avenue. He hesitated there on the corner, explaining how he should get back to work in his apartment on 16th street, just a couple of blocks uptown.

He was a criminal lawyer, apparently, and though young, just picked up by the Manhattan District Attorney's Office. Quite the prestigious assignment, she thought, though he assured her he was just starting out and was just one in over a dozen assistants in the offices. But he was eager, she could see, and he had a boyish charm about him that just seemed attractive to her. Biting his lip, he finally walked her the extra blocks west and over to 15th Street and the Jeanne d'Arc Boarding House, where she usually stayed when in town.

Never one to beat around the bush, Rita was still a bit surprised when she actually asked him to dinner for that night. She laughed at the comical look of shock; slack-jawed and eyes bulging as he sputtered response:

"Yes!"

They had been friends ever since.

She was looking forward to seeing him again, later that night, and—

"Hey," someone shouted, and Rita looked up. She hadn't been paying attention to her surroundings—rule number one in the big city—and she saw some heel charging down the street with a bag in hand, a purse, obviously not belonging to him. Not far behind she saw a woman screaming and waving her arms, calling for the police or anyone to help her. Some gutter, pickpocket had spotted her as some easy mark no doubt; an out-of-towner bumpkin on holiday with a huge bag to pilfer.

"Your mistake, pally," Rita cursed and gave chase while the rest of the street crowd stood looking in confusion.

The guy was quick—she had to give him credit—running fast and shoving aside pedestrians and shoppers along the street without a thought as he made his escape. She felt her adrenaline building as she dashed after him, leaping over an older woman with an overturned shopping cart and dodging a fallen businessman sprawled on the sidewalk. Luckily she was still dressed in her flight suit from the morning: jodhpurs and flat-heeled, high boots, a blouse and her leather jacket. Damn if she had to chase the file down in heels and a pencil-skirt.

She gained on him by the far corner but he dashed out into the surge of traffic on 6th Avenue without a care. Rita heard horns blaring and tires squealing as she followed with a quick glance. There was a crash downtown as the man turned and crossed Fourteenth to the opposite side. It was chaos as he dodged in-and-out of traffic and parked cars, finally dipping behind a crowded crosstown bus. Rita was almost right behind him though, bumping off the bus's front grill then shouldering through gawkers on the sidewalk. She spotted him again running back out into the street just a few yards ahead.

He darted in front of a motorcycle courier who was forced to turn abruptly, sending his cycle into a fierce slide and spilling off to roll onto the asphalt. Sparks flew with the skid and she saw her chance. She ran up to the churning cycle and hefted it back onto two wheels with a strained huff, revving the engine even as she slung a long leg over the Harley-Davidson RL 45. She gunned the motor and let it fly with a shriek, holding the machine steady as it roared forward, popping up onto the hind wheel but bringing her closer, faster to the thief.

Rita leaned into the wheelie as the man glanced back, a look of surprise on his face. She stood up on the pegs and forced the bike down, slamming the spinning front tire against the thief's back. He screamed in panic as he stumbled forward, trying to keep his footing, but finally spludding into the gutter in a heap. The purse went flying as she leapt from the cycle, letting it go to trundle and bounce, smashing into the back of a bulky sedan. She hit the sidewalk hard but rolled with the impact, thumping against a car at last and shaking her head trying to regain her bearings. She saw the snatcher doing the same, but she was quicker and scrambled to her feet, charging at him and jumping. Rita landed with a knee in his back, slamming him hard into the pavement.

"Yawww," he screamed, but she ignored him, shoving him down and wrestling against his struggles. He spat and cursed her as she drew back her arm. She heard bone crunch as her fist drove into his nose. Blood splattered with the impact and his head bounced back off the cement. He stared at her blankly as snotty scarlet gushed from his nostrils, his mouth flapping. She hit him again.

Rita sat astraddle over her would-be thief as he lay limp and unmoving beneath her. He was still breathing, which was good. She didn't need the hassle of dealing with the local flatfoots who were probably on the way. She heard the courier's motorcycle still rumbling out in the street and hoped the Harley wasn't too banged-up. It was a good machine—Clark Gable had one as she recalled—and with a little effort the courier would be back on the job with a story to tell. Looking up and breathing hard, she saw a crowd starting to gather around the scene. Time to go.

Rita untangled herself from the thug and got up, grabbing the nearby purse. She held the old bag and looked about at the mob of gawkers trying to spot the owner. At last she saw the woman frantically running up.

"Oh my god. Thank you! Thank you so much," the woman cried as she ran right up. Rita handed her the over-sized purse with a smile and the woman pulled it to her, hugging it tearfully. She was a bit older than Rita, in her thirties and plump, dressed rather plainly by her clothes, but nice in her pale blue skirt and sensible shoes. She was also quite pregnant.

"Are you all right?" Rita asked as the would-be victim started digging through her bag, nodding and breathing hard, "do you need to sit down?"

"No…" She gulped a deep breath, looking up again and smiling. Tears ran down her cherub cheeks. "I'm fine; just a bit out of breath. I was so worried. I just came from the bank. My rent money's in here and I needed to buy some things for the baby," she rubbed her stomach and held onto the swell, "it's all I have; Thank you!" The crowd around them was growing and Rita heard a police whistle sounding not too far away.

"You should shoulder your bag cross-body when in the city," Rita said with a reassuring smile and jiggling the strap on her own bag, "like this. And always pay attention to what's going on around you. We're still in a Depression, y'know, and times and people are desperate." The woman nodded.

"Yes, thank you! Thank you so much. I don't know how to repay you—" Rita waved her off.

"Forget it. Just make sure," she jerked a thumb back over her shoulder pointing at the groaning thief on the ground, "you press charges on that guy and get him arrested when the police finally show up. A couple nights in the slammer will be good for him and get him off the streets. Okay?" The woman nodded vigorously again.

"Yes, yes, of course I will," the woman agreed, staring daggers at the cutpurse. They both heard the police whistle again, closer now, so Rita turned to leave.

"Take care now," she said as the woman touched her arm.

"Aren't you staying? The police are coming and you're a hero." Rita grinned and stepped away, not wanting to get involved with police procedure and red-tape. She saw plenty of witnesses gathered now who would be willing to get their names in the papers.

"Naw," she dismissed, "I'm just a concerned citizen. Sorry," was all she offered hearing the police officer pushing through the crowd ordering people back out of the way as she started off west up the block towards 7th Avenue.

"At least tell me your name," the woman called after her.

"Radio Rita," she yelled back, just turning the corner, "at your service."

Out of sight, hopefully out of mind.

Delmonico's Restaurant
56 Beaver Street
Manhattan

"Bradley," Rita called out from the crowd gathered on the sidewalks in front of Delmonico's Restaurant. She waved, perhaps a bit too exuberantly for the ritzy snobs milling about her waiting—hoping—to get into one of the most exclusive eateries in the city, but she didn't care. Screw the rubes. She was happy to see Brad.

Up-and-coming Assistant District Attorney or not, she saw him light up when he saw her, waving just as enthusiastically as he made his way through the crowd. Men and women alike gave them dirty looks down their noses and she could hear the semi-hushed whispers from the gossiping gentry, no doubt derogatory, mumbles about the common riff-raff thinking they could get in anywhere above their stations. Rita ignored them as she always did.

Finally, her friend burst through the mob to stand before her. He was beaming with delight, and she just had to smile. He looked dashing in his slate-gray suit, off-the-rack no doubt, but obviously tailored to fit and appearing quite sharp. His wavy brown hair was slicked-back save for a long lock hanging over his eyes, not detracting from his handsome features, though she thought he looked a little haggard. Too much work and late hours, she imagined, as the rising star in the D.A.'s office. She felt that momentary spark again that initially caught her eye: young, intelligent and handsome. What girl wouldn't melt into those dark brown eyes?

And she was pleased to see her praise reciprocated as he looked her up-and-down, taking her in. She had napped and freshened up at the boarding house, which luckily had a room to let. She showered and made herself up, then dressed to the nines herself, wearing a slinky black, silk number which cost a small fortune. Not quite still in style, it hung low on the shoulder with a scooping neckline and cinched at the waist, hanging about mid-thigh with a slit up the left leg. It probably showed way too much skin and definitely too much thigh and stocking-top for a night with society, but she didn't care. She had dressed for Brad, not the snobs.

"You look fantastic," he exclaimed with a boyish crack in his voice, still standing at arm's length. "It's so good to see you again."

"Ditto on both counts," she returned and threw caution to the wind. She lunged forward and hugged her good friend, giving him a kiss on the cheek then taking a step back. He was blushing, bless him, and she could hear the murmurs start up from the gathering again. "I'm so glad we could get together."

"Me too," he agreed sheepishly, a finger trying to loosen his collar as he looked towards the closed doors of the restaurant. "I certainly wasn't expecting Delmonico's though. I doubt we'll get in. I don't have that much clout yet." Rita giggled and grabbed his hand.

"Trust me," she said as she dragged her companion through the crowd of hopefuls' right up to the main entrance. She heard the complaints as she shouldered past without a care to status and priority.

"Hey!"

"There is a line, lady."

"They won't let *her* in."

"Tramp!"

Rita ignored them all as she eyed the huge, oaken doors of polished wood, old gas torch sconces flickering to either side and eyeing the silver bell set back in a cubbyhole beside the entry. She reached right out and rang the bell.

It took a few moments but finally she heard the doors unlock and one opened a crack. A short man dressed in a fine, black tuxedo and tails stepped out onto the stoop, looking at the mob with disdain. He was frowning, looking all prim and proper, dripping venom without saying a word. She saw he was holding a small, leather-bound folder under one arm as he addressed the crowd:

"As I've said," he drolled with a sardonic twist, "our accommodations for the evening are filled. Unless you have a reservation," he tapped his ledger for emphasis, "you shall not gain entry. Please disperse." She felt Brad's hand on her arm as Rita stepped up a step to tower over the little man as he was about to disappear inside once again.

"Check your papers, Jeeves," she said, her smile never faltering, "I believe we're on your list." The short man somehow managed to look down his nose at her with a sniff, but he did look at his reservation sheets.

"I highly doubt that…*Miss*," he mumbled, "Name?"

"Bradley Morgan, Assistant DA," she stated proudly for all to hear, "party of two." He snorted as he scanned his papers then closed the folder.

"As expected I have no Morgan on my list," he snubbed with derision. "Perhaps you're mistaken. Try the Stork Club," he sniffed and was about to slam the door in her face when he finally made eye contact. His frown turned into a sneer as he opened his ledger again, looking at a smaller note.

"I don't suppose you are 'Radio Rita,'" he whispered, a note of slight disgust in his voice.

"All day, Charlie," she laughed, looping her arm in Brad's to bring him beside her. The man sighed.

"My name is Maurice, *Miss*," he corrected, snapping his folder shut, "and it seems you do have a standing invitation for the Chef's Table." She could almost hear him counting in his head trying to stay calm.

"If you will be so kind as to follow me."

"Sure, Maury," she jibed dragging a stunned Brad through the doorway, "lead on."

The man stepped slightly to the side and Rita heard the uproar of the crowd again as they were allowed in. She laughed.

"I don't believe it," Brad whispered leaning towards her ear, "how?"

"Stick with me, kid," she giggled, patting his arm. "I do get around."

Bradley Morgan laughed as the door slammed loudly behind them.

Dinner had been fabulous. Chef Pierre really outdid himself this time with his menu prepared especially for her and Brad. Maybe trying to score some brownie points with the DA's office and expand his clientele? She had mentioned Bradley's position on the train ride into the city. Or perhaps he was just showing off.

Whatever the reason, she was full, fit enough to burst with another bite. She looked down at her almost empty bowls and plates, just little bits of food remaining. She had heard somewhere years ago it was better decorum to almost clean your plate, but leave a little behind rather than wiping it clean. Leaving a few morsels showed the food was good but far too much to finish rather than appearing to be not enough and wanting more or something like that. Whatever, she was stuffed.

Pierre had been secretive about the night's menu, but she saw the remains of the things he purchased in the Green Market, the array of peppers catching her eye especially. She wasn't too surprised when her food arrived to find an Oriental stir-fry dish consisting of beef and broccoli with sliced carrots, red and green peppers, snap peas, and some long Asian noodles. She could taste dark soy sauce in the marinade along with a hint of Shaoxing wine, garlic, onion, brown sugar, and ginger. There was a huge bowl of steaming white rice for she and Brad to share as well as a small silver pot of coffee, and a finer china tea set filled with hot green tea: their choice. Of course, all the amenities and

"If you will be so kind as to follow me."

condiments littered the table. Pierre hadn't missed a trick and was definitely showing off.

Rita clacked her chopsticks chasing a bite of habanero pepper she spied around the bowl and saw her companion finally set his utensils on his plate with a sigh. He settled back into his plush leather chair with a contented smile looking at the remains of his more traditional dinner: a hefty T-bone steak, baked potato, and some type of green bean salad that had looked scrumptious. Unlike her, Bradley had eaten ravenously, devouring everything but the huge bone. He had even dabbed up the last of the mushroom gravy with his dinner roll. He pulled a cigarette case from his jacket pocket and plucked one free, offering one to her, which she declined. He lit up with a look of sheer contentment on his face.

"That was truly indescribable," he praised. "I just don't have the words. Your friend is a true Master."

"So, you liked that, huh," she grinned, wiping her brow of perspiration. Pierre knew she loved spice in her life and aimed to please with his pepper choices. "It was good," she agreed setting her chopsticks down again. No more. Brad nodded.

"I needed that… this whole night. I admit, I've missed a few meals and when I do remember to eat it's usually take-out from some greasy diner."

"They're keeping you busy at the DA's office I take it?"

He snorted."Busy's not the word for it. I'm the new boy so I get all the drudgery. But I've done a good job so they upped the ante with my latest case."

"Oh?"

"Well, I can't get too specific, but it's a Hit-and-Run Manslaughter involving a diplomat from the League of Nations. This little girl was out walking her dog with her mother late one night and chased the dog out into the street. She got hit and killed. Turns out the guy was drunk and getting," he leaned closer, whispering, "a blow-job.

"It turns out he has Diplomatic Immunity so there's a ton of red-tape, paperwork and legalese to wade through trying to get a conviction. I've been burning my candle on both ends with a bowl of midnight oil on the side ever since graduating Berkeley and moving out here. Food and sleep's a luxury these days, which is why I enjoyed this so much. Good food, better company. I needed the break."

Rita was about to comment when the wine steward appeared at the table carrying a bottle of Napoleon Brandy and a pair of snifters on a silver tray.

"Compliments of Chef Pierre," the steward announced, setting down the tray and presenting the bottle for Bradley's inspection. His eyes widened.

"*L'Esprit de Courvoisier*, 1811," he whistled softly, nodding to the steward. The man opened the temporary seal on the bottle and uncorked the stopper, offering it to Brad to sniff before pouring a small amount into a separate crystal glass. Brad swirled and sipped, struggling not to roll his eyes in pleasure. The cognac had been allowed to breathe before transferred to the decanter and Rita could tell it must be rich and fine by her friend's expression.

"That's excellent," Brad approved and the steward swiftly poured ample amounts into each snifter before stopping the decanter and bidding his leave with a slight bow. Brad waited for the steward to depart out of earshot before leaning in again.

"This brandy is over a hundred years old and costs probably a couple thousand dollars," he whispered in awe as Rita swirled her snifter. Her eyes boggled a bit at that news but she tried to hold her composure, mostly. "Just what kind of pull does your friend have here?"

"Pierre's a man of many talents and one of the most sought after chefs in the city," she shrugged, "at least from what I've heard. I figure Oscar Tucci wants to keep him on staff, so…"

"Well, thanks then to the owner and Chef Pierre for a most memorable and enjoyable evening." Brad raised his glass in toast and Rita did likewise, clinking hers to his.

"Cheers."

"Well, as I live and breathe," a new voice interrupted the moment and Rita cringed; she knew that voice, "the *fabulous*, Radio Rita."

Rita took a sip of her brandy, which had suddenly lost some of its appeal and looked up at the intruder. He was tall and handsome she supposed, in a swarthy sort of way, with dark, ruddy skin and slicked-back raven-black hair. He had a slim, pencil-thin mustache above his thick lips and piercing, dark brown eyes which always seemed to be burning into whatever he looked upon. Her in this case. As always there was a woman at his side; this time a pretty, platinum-blonde whose breast-size was probably larger than her I.Q. That's the way Wilbert "Blackie" Blackthorn liked his women; cute and clueless.

"Hello, *Wil*-bert," Rita half-greeted emphasizing his real name. His escort's big blue eyes seemed to focus for a moment as she looked up at him.

"Wilbert? I thought your name was Blackie?" Blackthorn grimaced at his obviously inebriated date.

"It is, Dear," he corrected, shushing her. She grinned happily and leaned on his arm.

Blackie Blackthorn gave her a grim look then turned his attention back to Rita. He sniffed once and glanced briefly at Brad, who was looking the other man up and down. Blackie smiled.

"I see Delmonico's opens their doors to all the riff-raff these days," he sniffed again. "I suppose I'll just have to take my business elsewhere from now on."

"I guess so, Wilbert," Rita countered looking at his date for the evening with a sweet smile. "I hear there's some good Gin-joints down in the Bowery that make a wicked pepper-steak. Your 'friend' might like that. Seems more her style."

"Oh, and allow me to introduce my date and good friend, Bradley Morgan," she said with pride. "He's a DA with the Manhattan offices." Rita looked at her friend and he grinned, understanding the sparring between two rivals. He stood, extending his hand, which Blackthorn eventually shook briefly. Not one to be overcome however, he quickly regained his composure.

"I do hope I'll see you at the race on Saturday," Blackie said with a smirk.

"Oh, I'll be there, Wilbert," she assured, "though you'll probably only be seeing my exhaust. I plan on winning that race, Wilbert. Ten thousand bucks will go a long way."

"Indeed," Blackthorn agreed, "but I plan on winning. My plane will prove far superior to yours."

"We'll just have to see come Saturday, Wilbert." Rita all but ignored him then, sipping at her brandy while Brad took the cue and took a long drag on his cigarette. "See you at Floyd Bennett."

"Yes," Blackthorn intoned as he nodded, trying to steer his companion towards the door. Rita and Brad watched the pair until they were out of the dining room, then Bradley chuckled.

"Well, he was certainly—" Rita cut him off.

"Arrogant, pompous, smarmy, slimy: take your pick. The list goes on and on and only gets worse." Bradley laughed, chaining a new cigarette. This time Rita took one as well. Blackie always rubbed her the wrong way.

"Problem is, he *is* a good pilot," she added, drawing on her cigarette, "but he likes to cheat. Can't prove it, but everybody knows it."

"And you really think you can beat him?"

"I think so," Rita said after a minute. Brad refilled their snifters and she took a drink. "I just don't know what he'll be flying. Howard assures me though; nothing can beat his H-1 Racer."

"Well, I'll be rooting for you from my apartment."

"Oh, I was hoping you might come."

Bradley shrugged. "Can't, sorry," he seemed sad. "This case I'm working on."

"I understand," she said, patting his hand on the table making him smile. "Just keep me in your thoughts."

"Always, Rita," he said taking a sip of brandy. "Always…"

Floyd Bennet Field
Marine Park
Brooklyn, New York

"Try it now, Rita."

At Monkey Parker's okay, Rita double-checked her flaps, ailerons, and joystick standby positions then flipped the ignition switches and spurred the Pratt & Whitney engine to life. The plane shuddered briefly—as all planes do at start up—and she heard the briefest sputter, but soon the motor was running clean and purring like a kitten.

Rita leaned out the open cockpit and yelled down to her mechanic: "Sounds good, Monkey!"

Standing off to the side and wiping his hands of grease on a filthy rag, Monkey Parker looked up and grinned madly.

"I think that got it," he shouted back. "Just the timing, like I thought." He ran back to the plane and climbed the short ladder resting against the fuselage before plunging a wrench into the depths of the housing. "Give it a little more juice, huh?"

Rita complied flipping the throttle control on the joystick increasing the flow of fuel through the carburetor. The engine roared loud and strong as Parker cranked on his wrench, tightening something. The roar swiftly quieted and smoothed as Rita felt the surge of power all around her. The Hughes H-1 Racer was straining at the leashes, wanting to fly free.

"Sounds good, Rita," a new voice shouted up from the far side of the plane. Rita saw the plane's inventor, Howard Hughes himself, reaching up to run a hand along the smooth, silver lines of the fuselage. He was handsome, Rita thought, dressed in a sharp, tailored suit and apparently not scheduled to race today, thank God. Her chances of winning would be next to nil if the engineer and record-setting pilot had the flying bug in his ear today. Rita hoisted herself up in the cockpit to better hear as Monkey closed-up the engine's housing.

She saw Hughes wasn't alone as he stepped back to the small crowd of people gathered about. They were all wearing light, business-style suits and dresses in the unseasonable warmth, so Rita figured they were somehow officially tied to today's airshow and festivities, the Pulitzer Trophy Race. Maybe judges or sponsors. She recognized Diane Pulitzer, publisher of the *New York World* newspaper and radio, heiress to the Pulitzer Media Empire, benefactor and founder of the race for her trophy and prize money. A handsome woman in her forties or fifties, Rita knew she was honest and fair in all her dealings, which were many.

She was speaking with the only other dignitary Rita recognized, though she doubted there was anyone in the New York vicinity who did not know the form and voice of Fiorello LaGuardia, popular and outspoken Mayor of New York City. Short and chubby, Rita knew he was one of the guest-judges for the day's events.

As Monkey removed his ladder and signaled, Rita shut down the engine and climbed out of the cockpit. She was already dressed for the upcoming air-race in her brown leather flight jacket, gloves and boots, loose jodhpurs, and a blouse. Her shoulder-length, red hair was pulled back to accommodate her flight cap and goggles later, and she had an unknown smudge of grease on her pretty face. She ducked under the cooling craft as Monkey dragged the hose from the fuel truck closer, taking a look at the tail's edge. Rita pulled off her gloves as she approached the group.

Hughes stepped right up for a quick kiss on the cheek and a hearty hug as always before stepping back a bit to introduce the entourage. Even putting names to the faces, she did not know the other four in the group. She was pleased to officially meet Pulitzer though, who she long admired, as well as the mayor, shaking hands all around.

"We're just making the rounds," LaGuardia explained, dabbing at his perspiration with a handkerchief. "Introducing ourselves to all the pilots and giving our best wishes." Always the politician.

"Howard insisted we meet you first though," Pulitzer added. "As you *are* flying his plane."

"And how's she doing, Rita," Hughes cut in, watching Parker hook up the fuel line.

"Running great and raring to go," Rita replied with a smile. "We were just finishing pre-flight when you came up. A final check." Hughes nodded and stepped back, looking over the length of his plane, loaned to Radio Rita for the race.

"That's fantastic," he praised with a satisfied grin. "And I know she's in good hands. It should be quite the spectacle."

He gestured towards the airfield and the course. The grandstands were nearly filled to capacity. Food booths were arranged near an area set aside for other companies with planes to display. It was quite the fair with people still streaming onto the grounds to partake of the booths of food, games, and presentations. Rita saw in the distance the pylons constructed marking the far end of the race course leading out over Jamaica Bay and all around the airfield and surrounding park. It wasn't a vast route, but the race consisted of several laps encircling the area; a 387-acre once-marsh now converted into the 'Gateway to the Greatest City in the World', or so they're hoping. High above she saw *Airship-27*, Hangar 27's signature zeppelin floating lazily in the pristine blue skies over the bay, no doubt manned by Captain Ron and the dedicated Hangar-27 crew. Always a thrilling sight, today it inspired her with confidence.

"Hopefully just a good, clean race," Rita added to which one of the group added: "Amen."

"We'd best get on about our rounds, Howard," another in the group urged looking at his pocket watch. "We're scheduled to start in about an hour, but with all the preliminaries and speeches..." A sly glance at LaGuardia. "Well…"

"Yes, yes," Hughes agreed. "Good luck, Rita. And remember; dinner's on me regardless of the outcome." He smiled amidst a round of "best wishes" from the rest, and the dignitaries were off. Rita watched after them a moment as they chatted walking towards the next staging area until she heard Monkey unfastening the fuel hose and locking down the equipment.

"All set, Rita," he proclaimed as he coiled the hose about its casing, flushing out the line. "I'll go get the tow truck and hook her up. We'll be ready to go in a few minutes."

"Sounds good," she agreed, slipping on her gloves again. The mechanic saluted then trotted off towards the maintenance hangar as Rita circled around the plane again, giving it her final scrutiny.

The sleek streamlining of the craft was paramount in the design, resulting in a clean and elegant aircraft. Rita knew many groundbreaking technologies were developed during the construction process, including individually machined, flush rivets that left the aluminum skin completely smooth and almost friction-free. The H-1 also had retractable landing gear to further increase the speed of the aircraft, including a fully retractable hydraulically actuated tail skid. It was fitted with a Pratt & Whitney R-1535 twin-row 14-cylinder radial engine of 1,535 cubic inches, which although originally rated at 700 horsepower, was tuned to put out over 1,000 horsepower. Howard's racing plane was fast, but she also knew it was designed to be converted between air racing and speed records with the set of short-span wings attached now, or a longer set for cross-country racing. The man was a genius for sure, but he was also a visionary.

As was she. And she supposed every female pilot felt the same. She could not begin to express the thrill she felt being able to fly free and push her abilities to their limits. It was exhilarating every time she got in the cockpit. Hearing the engine's roar and vibration, the rush of power as she commanded the craft in lifting off and soaring high, faster and faster, rolling, diving, the intense thrill of landing again in one piece. And to be a woman in this age of adventure, along with so many others, more and more, to be accepted and equal…

God, it was great to be alive.

Rita felt her anticipation and excitement growing as the rumbling sound of the old tow-truck approaching broke her from her reveries. Monkey parked the truck a few yards in front of the plane and scrambled out of the cab looking as anxious as she, caught up in the fever of the race. He unlatched the tow-cable and started hauling it back to the plane to hook up to the undercarriage.

"I've got this, Rita," he said ducking under the fuselage, "I'll give a yell when we're ready to roll."

"Thanks," Rita said patting the side of the craft and leaning in to give it a quick kiss for luck.

"Do good, baby," she whispered admiring her lipstick mark, "do good."

Radio Rita ran through the pilot's checklist once again with nervous anticipation building within her. She flipped all the switches by well-practiced rote; jiggling the throttle to open the fuel lines, tapping gauges, easing dials and preparing the H-1 Racer for take-off. Hughes had built his craft with the pilot's ease in mind and everything was within reach or a quick peripheral glance. All was well-marked and brightly lit; simple really compared to some planes she'd flown. If it flew half as well as it did in her initial test flights, it would be a dream.

Outside, Monkey gave his own one last inspection checking all the movable parts along the wings and tail section. Every piece he moved or adjusted signaled in the cockpit for Rita to comply, flipping another switch or easing a dial until perfect. A thumb's up from her and he moved on to the next with a grin. Everything was going well.

"So why are you so nervous, Rita," she whispered to herself.

Checking the time, Rita pulled off her leather pilot's cap and gloves to run a hand back through her fiery red hair. She was dripping with perspiration, probably from the excitement and anxiety, but it was also warm in the closed cockpit. *Indian Summer* had settled over the Tri-State for the last couple days making late October unseasonably warm. Everyone was hoping for a break, enjoying the warmth until the humidity settled in like a wet-blanket making everyone grouchy. Looking out across Jamaica Bay beyond the runway she could see dark smudges of clouds on the horizon, probably a storm coming off the Atlantic and hopefully some relief as well. But one never knew as it was New York with ever-fickle weather.

Trying to calm a bit, Rita waggled her hands and took deep breaths as she looked out to the other planes arranged along the starting line. There were four others, all larger than her own Racer but none the less impressive. On her right sat an *Aero A.200*—a Czech touring plane built for the *Challenge International de Tourisme* of 1934. A far larger, 4-seater it appeared streamlined and stripped down for today's race. She didn't recognize the pilot, though by his look of intensity as he double-checked the cockpit readings, she was certain the Aero was his baby.

To her left towards the grandstand sat three more planes; an old *Bernard H.V.42* modified racing seaplane with the water skids replaced by actual ground landing gear, and a *Caudron C.460* of Italian make which she learned won the *MacPherson Trophy* in '34. Both looked slick and well-built, trim and probably swift. She did not know those pilots either, though she could see the Caudron would be flown by another woman. She hoped to meet her and all her fellow pilots after the race. All but the fifth of course; Wilbert Blackthorn she knew all too well.

Blackie was situated in the farthest slot closest to the grandstands and standing in the open cockpit of his *Brown B-3 Racer* playing for the crowd. He stood waving all around, already taking bows and blowing kisses to the packed seats as his burly mechanic ran about his plane doing the preflight. Blackie seemed uninterested, gesturing wide to the spectator's approval. Rita could hear cheers and shouts of encouragement even with the din of the whining loudspeaker projecting Mayor LaGuardia's speech droning over all. She cranked open her triangular vent window to hear as well as feel some air circulating through the cab.

"The magnificent City of New York welcomes all our renowned guests international to our beautiful city for this great race. We hope by hosting this race, here on the grounds of one of America's first and foremost airports, *Floyd Bennet Field*, to better cement our ties with our European allies in these trying times. As our esteemed president, Franklin Delano Roosevelt mentioned to me recently..."

Rita took a deep breath through the side window then cranked it closed again, trying to tune out the mayor's speech. Always the showman, she had heard it all before. She wiped at her brow again and slipped on her gloves as Monkey slammed on the fuselage below the cockpit. She looked down to see him giving her a final thumb's up; all was ready. A quick salute and he gathered his tool bag up to jog off towards the staging area. Rita sighed, pulling on her cap once more and watching the dignitary's box for the final signal.

Mayor LaGuardia rambled on but finally introduced Diane Pulitzer to the crowd amidst clattering applause. She said something to the mayor and stepped up to the microphone holding a furled flag in hand. She welcomed everyone; pilots and spectators alike as Rita pulled her flight goggles in place, watching and listening.

"...but I think we've all had enough ado," she announced as she unfurled the solid green starting-flag. "So... Pilots, start your engines!"

Rita flicked the ignition switch and tickled the throttle as she urged the H-1

She looked down to see him giving her a final thumb's up.

to life. She felt the engine kick on; the initial shudder of the plane as the propeller fluttered to life and began to spin. Within seconds the electric starter powered the motor to full strength with all the gauges reading prime conditions. The roar of the other planes as well as her own drowned out the cheers of the crowds as Rita angled the control stick awaiting the final signal. She could see the intensity on the faces of her neighboring pilots as all eyes turned towards the starter's box awaiting the final signal.

Rita licked her lips.

Diane Pulitzer raised her flag high overhead, briefly glancing at her fellow dignitaries then eyeing each of the planes. All were raring to go. Her smile widened as she flourished the flag overhead—three flamboyant waves to get everyone's attention—then dramatically cut the flag down in a sweeping gesture whipping it wildly.

"GOOOooooo..."

All the planes seemed to jump forward at once and began the long charge down the runway. She heard what must have been the initial sound of a starter's pistol explode over the roar of the engines and cheers of the crowd, but she couldn't see the source. She could see Jamaica Bay sparkling in the distance some 4000 feet away; a swift end in the icy water for any planes that could not get airborne. Rita was not worried as she adjusted her controls keeping one eye on her dials and gauges, another on her fellow pilots to maintain space between the planes, and yet another on the fast-approaching bay. Howard assured her the H-1 would power fast and reach top speed long before the runway ended.

Far to her left she could see Blackie's Brown rising higher as he pushed for the advantage. He was riding close to the wide runway's edge and the grassy field beyond. Whoever set up the race's course had chosen Floyd Bennet's longest and widest runway for the start as it was better equipped for larger planes like transports and flying-boats. A good idea as the planes were in tight formation as they vied for position. Rita cursed as Blackie's aircraft raised fully gaining the initial jump on the others and taking a quick lead.

Another explosion sounded somewhere behind her and Rita immediately thought she was having engine trouble. The gauges read in perfect order though and there was no telltale vibration. Then she saw in the small, compact-mirror she had affixed to the upper-left of the cockpit to give her a view of the plane's fuselage outside, a plume of black smoke rising back at the starting line. She kept peeking at the rear-reflection as her gaze swept the view before her and saw one of the other planes—the Bernard she thought—turned slightly off-kilter with smoke billowing from its engine casing. Rita didn't know the pilot or crew of the craft but could not understand why the plane was having sudden problems. A faulty part, maybe, or something they missed in preflight; something else?

Rita cursed as Blackie pulled further ahead and the Caudron lifted into the air. She adjusted the flaps with her foot pedals and increased the airflow as she pressed back into her leather-clad chair pulling the stick between her legs.

The plane bounced then bounced again.

"C'mon..." she whispered and finally felt the thrill as gravity loosened its grip and her racer took to the air.

The runway fell away beneath her as she poured on the speed a good 1000 feet from the barricades at the edge of the water. Blackie was easing out quickly and the Caudron was even with her. The Aero was right behind though, picking up speed and trying to catch up. Still pulling the stick back to her she started to gain altitude, quickly rising now above the other planes trying to keep flying space away from the other craft.

And suddenly she was above the blue waters of Jamaica Bay. She retracted the landing gear as she saw the far marker approaching swiftly and started her wide turn to bank to the right, angling the plane for a close pass. The Brown, still in the lead, was almost skimming the surface of the water to cut close to the tall tower set up on one of the tiny, neighboring islands. Blackie was flying low to the ground and ignoring his other competitors without a care to safety, as always. But she was catching up.

She leaned into the turn touching the control to her thigh as she brought the plane about to follow the shoreline and the grassy edges of the field heading towards the next tower. The Aero pulled a tight turn as well, right on her tail as the Caudron pulled just a bit ahead. Biting her lower lip she eased the stick forward to level out the plane and poured on more speed.

It was a long stretch to the next marker and turn so now was the time to pick up speed and close the distance. Once the H-1 was free to really roll, Rita closed the flaps and ailerons to reduce friction once she achieved her desired height and the airfoil was once again sleek and smooth. The H-1 seemed to ease forward; pulling out from the Aero and easing past the Caudron. Blackie was still ahead and dropping lower, just a few feet over the water. He was throwing caution to the wind she supposed, not caring about his neighbors or his own craft. She saw the Caudron following Blackie's lead slipping through his slip-stream for the extra lift and pulling past her again as the pilot took the outside.

Blackie rounded the second marker low and tight; the Brown rolling into the sharp turn with the right wing actually skimming the top of the water. He controlled the sudden drag however, expertly adjusting the yaw to keep the plane from cartwheeling into the drink and leveling out. Rita and the Caudron were right behind though, maybe two lengths; she still above with the other female pilot lower and shifting behind the Brown again. She was good, Rita thought, Marion McKeen; the other woman pilot in the race.

The Aero was pulling left, almost even with her tail now as they all surged forward towards the third marker-tower. The Brown was losing ground at last as the Caudron came up almost even with him again and right on Blackie's tail. He quickly shifted the plane to block the Caudron but Rita was too far above and gaining ground moving to his left.

The third tower was at the far edge of the field and she could now see the skyline of Manhattan in the distance; its tall towers scraping the sky and looking glorious. She could see *Airship-27* high above in the distance, well away from the course, hanging lazily in the blue. She saw too the speck of another plane—a biplane by the look—far and away over New Jersey. Rita poured it on.

They all rounded the third marker together, almost in 'Fingertip Formation' with the starting line the next goal and marking the first lap. Rita saw Blackie pulling out again as he maneuvered dangerously close to the Caudron, forcing the other plane to veer. He was up to his usual dirty tricks, making McKeen drop back to avoid a collision. Smart of her but Rita hated Blackie's under-the-table tactics.

All the planes surged low past the grandstands pushing their airspeed. She could see the crowd watching and cheering them on, though she could not hear them over the roar of the engine. A brief glimpse caught Diane Pulitzer waving them on for the second lap and she saw the Bernard still on the runway spewing smoke. The field's fire-engine was pulling on scene with the fire-fighters dragging out the long hoses as the plane's mechanic frantically sprayed gouts of *pearl ash* from a metal fire-extinguisher. The pilot was standing off to the side looking defeated and out of the race.

The four remaining aircraft surged forward in the longest stretch once again, starting their second lap. Rita moved up beside the Caudron and even with the Brown, the three planes vying for the lead. Rita was pushing the H-1 to its limits and almost at its recorded top airspeed of 300 MPH. The plane was running smoothly though with no issues on any gauge. She dropped the racer down and urged it to do better, pushing it on.

She saw the Aero coming up at the marker taking the inside lane as it attempted a very sharp turn to get in front. She saw the plane was too low immediately as it banked and the wingtip dipped deep into the bay. It hit hard and plowed into the waters, tumbling wing-to-wing in a tight spin, cartwheel-like. She listened and glanced in her mirror but did not see or hear an explosion as she sped on; that was good. She hoped the pilot was okay as the remaining planes rounded the first marker a second time and rushed on.

The three remaining craft were vying for the lead now; almost neck-and-neck with Blackie still slightly ahead. Whenever she or McKeen tried to pull past, Blackie was still up too no good, trying to cut them off and hold them back. Rita pulled back on the joystick to get above the Brown as she checked her airspeed; 320 MPH. Now was not the time to stall. She saw the Caudron dipping lower and racing faster, close to the Brown but just under him.

Whether by chance or deviousness Rita saw Blackie's plane roll slightly so the tip of his wing tapped McKeen's. She saw sparks in the friction and the Caudron banked sharply heading at the ground. She tried to watch but the other plane fell back with distance and out of sight as she raced forward.

"And now we're two," Rita whispered as she poured on the speed and into the lead. She caught a brief glimpse of Blackthorn cursing as he did the same,urging the Brown on. They turned about the second tower; flags whipping atop in their passing.

They were even as they finally approached the grandstands again. Pulitzer waved another flag madly for them to see; white and signaling the final lap of the race. She and Blackie fought for the lead as she pulled on the stick to get away from him and his tricks, fighting the yaw and torque, not wanting to lose control. Blackie eased the Brown closer as his speed increased, up to something.

They rounded the first marker again, side-by-side and as she leveled out she saw the Caudron again coming up swiftly from behind. McKeen had pulled her craft out of the enforced dive, thankfully not crashing and trying to get back into the race. She was swiftly picking up speed.

Heading back towards the edges of the field, Blackie turned tight about the second tower and veered beyond trying to cut her off. Rita pulled to the right and tried to gain some space but Blackie shot in front of her again with his tail on her nose. He was trying to force her down as he let off the thrust coming above her propeller. In desperation, Rita veered to the right to get away but the Brown was right at her side and moving in. Rita bit on her lip and pulled hard on the control.

The H-1 screamed in protest at the sudden strain, shaking a bit but otherwise handling beautifully. She forced the plane into an extremely tight roll passing close over the Brown. She saw clear blue sky then a field of green before she managed to level-out on Blackie's far side. She saw her rival panicking in his cockpit at the abrupt, crazy move she made, but it worked. Blackthorn dove slightly to get away but he was too close to the ground. His landing gear touched and immediately his plane slowed and he suddenly pulled up, adjusting and almost stalling.

Rita burned past as they passed the third marker, now approaching the finish line, taking the lead. She could see the Brown trying to gain speed and catch up again but saw too the blur of the crowd ahead, swiftly approaching and becoming more distinct. Diane Pulitzer was in the starter's box holding out her checkered flag ready to declare the winner, all the other dignitaries on their feet and cheering. Rita licked her lips as she neared, lowering the landing gear. She was going to win.

Out of nowhere she saw the Caudron overhead and passing. She looked at her airspeed and saw she was pushing 350 MPH and could not imagine how fast the other plane was going. She fingered the throttle full-out for a burst of fuel and dipped her craft down heading for a landing. Rita was again neck-and-neck with the Caudron now slightly falling back.

Then ahead…

Even as both craft dropped in a slight stall, Pulitzer waved her checkered, black-and-white flag frantically as both planes sped over and past the finish line, touching down almost simultaneously. Rita killed the engine as she bounced along the runway, shutting down the power and adjusting the plane's instruments with McKeen running right at her side doing the same. Rita pulled off to the right of the runway once she slowed enough out into the grass as the Caudron centered on the tarmac finally coming to a stop and turning sharply almost at the barricades.

Rita leaned back into her seat with a long, deep sigh. She was still charged with adrenaline and shaking as she pulled up her flight goggles, fidgeting with the buckle of her flight cap. She pulled the leather cap off and tossed it to the side watching the far end of the runway and the Caudron to make certain Marion McKeen was all right. She could just barely see the other female pilot's shadowy form moving about in the cockpit as the canopy flipped open. McKeen stretched and stood up, looking around and Rita let out another long sigh.

Rita heard the sound of fire engines and only then remembered the others in the race. She popped open her own canopy and lifted it away to stand and look back at the field. She saw Blackthorn's Brown just over the finish line, the man himself waving at the crowd and garnering attention. He seemed none the worse for wear, but beyond she saw the Bernard being hooked up to a tow-truck; its engine casing open but no longer smoking and the plane's crew standing nearby gesticulating wildly in heated debate. All seemed fine as the fire engine started rolling her way.

She looked about for the downed Aero scanning the bay where she thought it went down. Finally she spotted a United States Coast Guard Rescue Cutter in the waters beyond the first marker. There was a tugboat as well as smaller skiffs swarming about the downed plane preparing to try to haul it to dock. The cutter signaled with a loud bellow of its horn that all was well and the pilot apparently safe; thank god.

Rita climbed out of her cockpit as the fire engine slowed near her just long enough to drop off two passengers. Monkey Parker and Howard Hughes were soon running towards her; the firetruck picking up speed again, heading for the Caudron. Rita stepped onto the wing of the H-1 and jumped down to the ground as the pair arrived, shouting.

"Rita!"

"My god! are you all right?"

"Lordy!"

"I'm fine," Rita assured her friends as they fawned over her for a moment; hugging and patting her shoulder. Finally though Monkey's anxious curiosity got the better of him and he ran over to the H-1 and pried open the engine housing. He backed up from the burst of heat and steam with a whistle as he peered inside. She had pushed the plane to its limits at least matching Howard's recorded airspeed of 350 MPH, though she suspected she beat him. He was understandably curious as well, but he kept his attention on Rita.

"Are you sure," he asked again and she nodded.

"I'm fine, really."

"Well, that last stunt you pulled was breathtaking, rolling over the Brown like that. I didn't realize the old H-1 could manage something like that at those speeds. All three of you were neck-and-neck, right down to the wire."

"And what about the other pilots who went down," she asked looking again at the Aero bobbing out in the bay, "everyone okay?"

"They're both fine," Hughes said following her gaze. "The Coast Guard was already patrolling in Jamaica Bay and was on the scene in seconds. They fished Russ Thaw out of the drink; cold and wet but otherwise A-Okay. I don't know about the plane."

"And the Bernard?" Howard shrugged.

"They're saying engine trouble, but I don't know. Leon Atwood, the pilot, said he heard a 'pop' and the engine started smoking. Grease and oil was burning on the motor, caught fire and the heat and pressure caused an explosion. He was fine; cursing like a longshoreman of course, but otherwise unharmed. Luckily Brooklyn's Bravest were on scene and got the fire out before it took the whole plane or caused further damage."

"That's great," Rita said truly glad. She knew it would probably take some time to determine what exactly happened with the Bernard, but Rita had her suspicions. "And Blackie?"

"Mad as hell," Hughes laughed and gestured towards the Brown and the man in question. Rita saw him still playing the crowd. "He got nothing he didn't deserve though, from what I saw, anyway. You really put him in his place."

"Hey!"

Rita and Howard both turned at the shout, looking down the runway and saw the final pilot jogging their way. Marion McKeen was dressed in leathers like Rita: a flight jacket and boots, slacks and a tee shirt. Her wavy brown hair was matted down from her pilot's cap and sweaty about her shoulders. She seemed fine though, Rita thought as she rushed up, a little smudged but unhurt.

"Marion," Howard exclaimed as he stopped her short and grabbed her arms looking her up and down. "You're okay?"

"I'm good, Howard," she said, "I'm good, but I wanted to check on her. That was quite the maneuver you made. I'm impressed." Hughes remembered his manners and gestured at Rita who stepped closer.

"I'm glad you're both all right, so let me introduce…"

"Radio Rita," McKeen said with enthusiasm, extending a hand, "she hardly needs an introduction, Howard. I'm just sorry we didn't have time to meet before the race." Rita smiled and shook McKeen's hand.

"Likewise," she agreed, "and just as impressed. I've been a fan since you joined the racing circuit. And the way you kept that Caudron going after Blackie's chicanery; amazing."

"It's a great plane," Marion said wistfully, looking back down the runway as Brooklyn Fire checked over the aircraft, "and hopefully it'll fly again."

"And I look forward to competing with you again, when you do. It was a great race."

"Speaking of which," Marion paused looking between Rita and Howard, both women turning to Hughes.

"Who won," they asked in unison. Howard Hughes laughed.

"And in 1st place," Diane Pulitzer announced over the microphone, "I present the winner of the *Pulitzer Trophy*; Marion McKeen!"

The crowd went wild as the publisher of the *New York World*, handed over the trophy, and an enlarged mock-up of the prize check; $9,500. Marion accepted with a gracious wave to the stands amidst cheers and applause, cradling a bouquet of flowers in her arm and holding the trophy high for all to see. Rita applauded and cheered as loudly as the rest. It had truly been a photo-finish at the wire as the H-1 and the Caudron crossed the line within a split second of one another. Apparently Pulitzer had one of her paper's best shutterbugs at the finish line though, one 'Stubby' Stubbins snapping pictures throughout the race and he caught the final moment on film. Marion had crossed the line first with the slimmest margin; ahead by the extension of her plane's propeller.

Cameras flashed as Marion pulled Rita up onto the upper platform of the winner's stand and raised both their hands together in victory. Rita flushed with excitement and acclaim, both women waving to the crowd as Pulitzer led the applause.

Rita wished she had won, of course; that prize money would have gone a long ways at Hangar-27, but she was happy for Marion. She won a well-deserved victory, and Rita's 2nd place award of $4,375 was nothing to sneeze at. It would do well towards paying off some bills and improving their equipment.

She saw the other pilots standing off to the side applauding their success; all but Blackie Blackthorn. The 3rd place podium stood empty; Blackthorn apparently slipping away in disgust over his defeat, a sore-loser amongst all his other slimy faults. No great loss.

Finally though, the closing ceremony wound down and Rita and Marion stepped off the platform. More congratulations as they made their way through the crowd on the field, shaking hands and accepting their accolades as they walked off towards the hangars in the distance. Rita saw Chef Pierre awaiting their approach.

"Ladies," he said, first shaking Marion's hand then giving Rita a quick hug. "A fantastic race and a well-deserved win to both of you. We're not done yet though," he smiled.

"I should check on my plane," Marion begged him off but Rita touched her arm to pause her.

"What do you mean, Pierre?"

"Well, you're both invited to a special dinner at the hangar. Go check out your plane, of course; first things first, but in an hour or so, expect a mouth-watering feast in honor of your victory." He glanced at Rita. "I've got steaks on the grill and shrimp on the 'barbie' with all my Southern cuisine on the side; barbequed potatoes, corn-on-the-cob, mac and cheese, with plenty of peppers," he winked at Rita. "All for you. As soon as Captain Ron and crew dock, dinner will be served."

Marion waved the man off. "I shouldn't," she said, "should I?"

Radio Rita shielded her eyes with a smile as she looked up to see the *Airship-27* zeppelin hovering low over the outskirts of the field casting lines to dock. The sun was getting fat and red as it dropped towards the horizon beyond New Jersey. Clouds were rolling in on a breeze that had popped up off the Atlantic, pushing out the humidity.

"Red sky at night," she whispered turning towards Marion.

"Do come back," Rita urged with admiration, "the dinner tonight will be the real prize." Marion laughed.

"I promise."

Rita watched as her fellow pilot and hopefully new friend headed off into the hangars to check out her plane. She was proud to have competed with her, and knew she would again. There were plenty of races upcoming, maybe even the Nationals in Cleveland next year. She vowed to be there…

And Radio Rita would win.

Count on it!

THE END

The Hughes H-1 Racer is a racing aircraft built by Hughes Aircraft in 1935. Using different wings, it set both a world airspeed record and a transcontinental speed record across the United States. The H-1 Racer was the last aircraft built by a private individual to set the world speed record; most aircraft to hold the record since have been military designs.

The Second Try

When Airship-27 Productions first announced their intentions of creating an anthology about their Mascot and Flagship Heroine, Radio Rita, I was interested to say the least. So too it seemed was everyone else, and with good reason.

Radio Rita was introduced as a member of Hangar-27's crew; a sexy and statuesque, fiery redheaded pilot and radio-operator who was also a Pulp Hero and adventurer. Ron Fortier would often share her words of wisdom through Airship-27's updates along with the imageries of Rob Davis and Vargas among others. Over the months her popularity grew, so it was only natural, Ron would announce his plans for a book of her collected adventures. With limited information and background offered, the anthology would contain four short stories about Rita; her tales as a hero and pilot in a Pulp setting. Needless to say, Ron sparked a fire of appeal which grew into a blaze and those first four slots filled quickly.

Thus came: *The Adventures of Radio Rita Volume I.* With fantastic tales from Teel James Glenn, Samantha Lienhard, Gene Moyers and Mel Odom accompanied by artists Rob Davis (interiors) and Ted Hammond (cover artist), Radio Rita exploded on the Pulp scene. With her popularity growing and desire to write about her building, again it was only a matter of time before Volume II was announced.

I shamefacedly admit I was a little slow responding to Volume I. I wanted to do it, but other life-commitments took precedent at the time. I did jump onboard for the second anthology. My first attempt however fell a little short; rejections are a part of every writer's life. It was a good story it seemed, but Ron Fortier explained it was not quite what he was looking for, and suggested I give it another go. Undaunted, I tried again.

After a little thought, another tale soon came to me, and when I started writing the pages just seemed to fill of their own accord. Always one to step up to a challenge given a great character with a rich, open background and world to play in, *The Great Race* swiftly fell into place; written, edited, fact-checked and presented to Ron, I apparently hit the nail squarely on the head with my second attempt within a few days. He loved it and it was accepted for *The Adventures of Radio Rita Volume II*, which you hold in your hands.

If you are reading this essay first, STOP! Go read the stories in the volume, mine and the others. I don't think you'll be disappointed. If you have read them, let us know; we're all part of those 'Starving Artists' you used to hear so much about. Write a review; good or bad, we want to know and we appreciate your support, thoughts and interest. And above all…

Enjoy!

CURTIS FERNLUND —was born May 15th, 1962 in Medford, Oregon, just a few miles north of the California border where he grew up with his parents and sister. He was raised there and went to school, worked and played until 1984 when he loaded up a U-Haul with most of his worldly belongings and drove cross country with three of his friends, eventually settling in Brooklyn, New York. A few years later he met his soul mate, Erica, and moved to Manhattan to live with her where they spent eighteen wonderful years together until her passing in 2006.

Arriving in Manhattan, he was hoping to get a career in the comic book industry as an artist, and though he did get some work published on occasion elsewhere he could not break into that field. He turned his focus to writing then, and that in Fan Fiction on the still developing Internet, as he had always been a comic book fan as well as of the older Pulp genre and a role-play gamer. After dozens, if not hundreds of stories posted on the Internet, another life goal was achieved, and he became a published paid author, thanks to Ron Fortier, Airship 27 and Erica, who always had faith in him.

Now over three decades later, older and hopefully wiser he's back living in Eugene, Oregon, doing the best he can and of course, writing.

To read more of his work, go to Airship 27 (airship27hangar.com):

"Kiri: Night of the Mist" in *Mystery Men (& Women) Volume 3,*
ISBN: 978-0615725994

"Kiri: Flight of the Valkyr" in *Mystery Men (& Women) Volume 6,*
ISBN: 978-1946183873

"Kiri: Rise of the Bund" in *Mystery Men (& Women) Volume 7,*
ISBN: 978-1953589125

The Queen of Escapes,
ISBN: 978-0615903866

Pick Up

by Gene Moyers

"Rita, can I have a word?"

The tall, redheaded woman and her companion stopped and turned. Both wore oil-stained khakis with the sleeves rolled up. His blonde hair was cut short while her long hair was pulled back in a ponytail. The good-looking young woman looked surprised for an instant before replying, "Sure, Rob." She turned and handed an oily, complicated looking, metal unit to her companion and said, "Go on ahead, Mike. I'll catch up."

Squadron 13's youngest pilot smiled and replied, "Sure, Rita." He then continued across the dusty runway toward a large wooden hangar whose wide doors were rolled back. Rita turned and walked toward the wood frame building that passed for headquarters here on the dusty airstrip just outside of Laredo, Texas.

Awaiting her in the door way was the solid figure of Rob Davidson, Squadron 13's second in command. Pulling an oily rag from her pocket, Rita was wiping her hands as she reached him, "What's up, Rob?"

Davidson was a solid, man, bigger than the dapper figure of the Squadron's skipper. He wore his hair slicked back from his high forehead, accenting his magnificent, waxed moustache. He was a pleasant man, well-liked and respected by everyone in the squadron. He nodded and asked, "How are the repairs on the Orion going?"

"We've got the carburetor rebuilt and we were just going to replace it. Then we'll do a run up and see if she's running any smoother."

Rob stepped to one side and motioned her into the building. He followed her, closing the door and asked, "Can Mike handle the repairs?"

In the large briefing room and general pilot hangout, Rita pulled a rag from her pocket, leaned against a table and said, "Sure, I guess. He's got a good feel for machinery. Better than me, maybe."

"Good. Because I've got something else for you. Something we need to get on right away."

Surprised, Rita left off wiping her hands and looked quizzically at Rob, "I thought things were kind of quiet, what with everybody off to the four winds."

"Yeah, it was supposed to be, but things have changed. We're short-handed and something has come up. You know that Dave Parsons is supposed to be on leave?"

"Sure. That's what he said before he left."

"Well, that's a little bit of fiction that the skipper cooked up. Actually Dave is on detached duty down in Mexico."

Rita raised an eyebrow, "Mexico? What's he doing down there?"

Rob, looked thoughtful, "Keep this under your hat, but he's doing some undercover work checking into some smuggling."

Rita was interested now, "Smuggling what?"

"Guns."

"Guns? Wow! Who would smuggle guns into Texas. There are more guns than people around here. Even my landlady's got a gun."

Rob looked solemn, "For a while now, serious amounts of guns have been coming across the border. And not just your everyday social guns. We're talking military rifles by the crate, heavy machine guns with enough ammunition to fight battles and explosives too."

Rita pursed her kissable lips and whistled softly, "Ahhhh! I'll bet that's got some people worried."

"It has. We got word from up north to look into it. So, Ron sent in Dave Parsons under cover. He's been snooping around down in northern Mexico for a week now."

"So his leave was just a cover. Has he found anything?"

"Up until now, no. He checks in every day by coded telegram. So far, everything's been negative; until this morning. We got word from him that he's got information and needs a ride out.

Rita perked up, "Ride?"

"Yep, his message indicated urgent; so we need to send someone in to pick him up, pronto."

Rita smiled, and touched a finger to her chest, "Me?"

Rob nodded, "With 'Wish' off flying patrol for the *Santa Fe*, up north, it's just you, me and Mike. Ron, Nick and Jake aren't scheduled in with the new blimp for another three days."

Rita shook her head, "Just what are we going to do with a blimp, in Texas?"

Rob looked thoughtful, "Well, since war's broken out in Europe, the powers that be are getting nervous about German submarines. You know they sank a British carrier with torpedoes south of Ireland last month. Anyway, the government's producing a lot of the new K class blimps and somebody thinks we can use one. So, once Ron gets back with it, you'll be getting training on it too."

Rita shrugged, "How hard can it be? They're slower than molasses."

"You might be surprised. They are actually very versatile. They're great for patrol and they are very quiet. Great for missions where surprise is important. But we don't have it yet, so you're flying the down to Mexico, today."

"Today."

"Today. Dave's telegram indicated urgency. If he's got hot intelligence, we need to get it back here, pronto."

"So, where am I going?"

Rob beckoned her across the room. She followed him where a large map was tacked to the wall. It covered most *Texas* and a good bit of northern *Mexico*. Leaning in, he got close to the map and after a second punched a finger hard on the map, "You're going, here."

Rita leaned in and looked the area over. About 120 miles south southeast of Laredo was Monterey, the largest city in northeast Mexico. A major rail line ran south and east from there, through Cuidad Victoria to Tampico on the Gulf Coast; a major port. Rob was indicating a small town along the railway near Cuidad Victoria; San Rosario. She looked the area over critically. It was deep in the mountainous Sierra Madre range of mountains. The altitude was high, maybe three or four thousand feet.

She spoke thoughtfully over her shoulder to Rob, "Rough territory. You think the smuggled guns are coming through there?"

"Maybe. It's on a rail line from the coast to Monterey. And there are a couple of main roads running north to the border not to mention lots of minor roads and dirt tracks. It might be a good place to waylay shipments off the railroad. That's what the intel suggested and it looks like Dave's found something."

"What exactly did his telegram say?'

"He was using innocent sounding code words but he indicated he had important info and needed immediate removal. If everything was normal, he would have taken a train out just like he went in. Asking for air pick up means he's onto something."

Rita looked thoughtful. Rob could see the wheels turning in her mind. She spoke deliberately, "That's nearly three hundred air miles. It's in the mountains and could be windy. What's the weather supposed to be like?"

"Nothing major for the next few days. Forecast is clear but windy throughout northeast Mexico."

"Hmmn, so what am I flying? Wait! There is an airfield in this town, right?"

"Dave says there's a day only field. No regular air service just refueling for local planes. That's mining country and a lot of companies have small planes. And you're taking the Vega. It has the range and was built for long distance work. You'll have to do all your own navigation but you're up to speed on that. That's another reason I'm sending you. Mike's got limited cross country experience."

"Charts?"

"I'll have everything ready in a few minutes. You better go get cleaned up."

Rita rubbed her hands together and smiled, “Right. Back in a Jif!”

She turned whistling, ‘In the Mood’ and hustled across the room and out the door. The slightest trace of smile on his face, Rob shook his head and turned for his office.

An hour and a half later Rita stood close to Rob. Twenty yards away the Lockheed Vega idled noisily. She leaned in close to hear Rob as he yelled to be heard over the racketing of the 400 hp Prat t& Whitney R-1340 engine, it’s nine-foot propeller a blur. Rob handed over a briefcase yelling, “Everything you’ll need is in there; air charts, details of the town and airfield. We telegraphed Dave back this morning that pick up would be this afternoon. He should be waiting for you at the airfield. You have plenty of range to get there and back without re-fueling. Hopefully, you’ll be back shortly after dark. We’ll man the radio and be listening for you. Let us know and when you’re close and we’ll turn on the field’s lights.”

Rita nodded, “Got it! Should be an easy flight. I’ll see you soon.” She turned and trotted toward the idling aircraft. Climbing up into the fuselage she waved and pulled the cabin door closed. Rob watched her work her way forward past the cabin windows to the cockpit. He stepped back as he saw her head appear in the cockpit side window. A minute later the engine revved and Rita taxied the big ship out toward the runway. At the end of the runway she paused. The sound of the engine wound up to a snarl and the Vega rolled down the runway faster and faster. It lifted off cleanly, Rita letting it climb away at an easy rate. At a thousand feet she turned lazily and flew back across the airfield, waggling her wings gently before setting out southward.

Adjusting power and fuel, Rita gradually let the big Vega climb. Reaching to her right she picked up her map. The large air map covered northeastern Mexico including the border area of Texas. She had folded it back upon itself to give herself a manageable, handheld view of her route. San Rosario, her destination, was along the railway, south of Cuidad Victoria. The course was about 170 degrees, just east of south. Setting down the map on the starboard side her seat, Rita scanned her instruments. She was climbing past three thousand feet. She adjusted her heading and noted her cruising speed of 140 knots.

Craning her head she leaned to her left, and dipped that wing slightly. The Rio Grande flowed south here; she was paralleling it into Mexico. The lowlands here were fairly well populated and the scrublands were broken up by many small and medium patches of green indicating irrigated farmlands. Rita then rolled the Orion to the right. Ahead and on that side the distant Sierra Madre

Oriental mountains dominated the skyline. Rolling the wings back level Rita scanned her instruments. Everything seemed normal: oil temp, oil pressure, manifold temperature.

The Vega's cockpit was wide and comfortable. Too wide in Rita's opinion. There was room for a second seat up front but instead the Vega's comfortable pilot's seat was in the center of the aircraft. Its seatback was actually the door leading to the cabin and its five seats. The problem was, with the pilot seat centrally located; Rita did not have good visibility out of the cockpit side windows. She could see upwards or at her level but she had to roll the aircraft over to see downwards. This was annoying enough but the vison forward wasn't any better. Although mounted high, the cockpit forward view was still restricted by the big Pratt & Whitney Wasp radial engine.

To her mind though, these were the Vega's only faults. Otherwise, she was a fine ship to fly. Nearly as big as the squadron's Shrikes, the Vega was smoother, quieter and much easier to fly. The enclosed cockpit was big and the seat quite comfortable. She was lighter on the controls than a Shrike, rolled faster and had a comfortable control wheel rather than a stick. Altogether, Rita found the Vega a pleasure to fly. Its only drawback was it was made for passenger transport over long distances, not speed. Many aviators had made record setting flights in the Vega, Amelia Earhart and Wiley Post among them.

Reaching her cruising altitude of five thousand feet, Rita leveled out and leaned back to enjoy her flight south. Picking up the map she scanned her planned route. South from the border were lowlands for nearly two hundred miles. Then the land gradually rose into the highlands before reaching the Sierra Madre Oriental.

San Rosario was a small town deep in the mountains south southeast of Ciudad Victoria. Since it would be hard to navigate directly to San Rosario, Rita was aiming to cut the rail line and follow it to Ciudad Victoria and thence down the rail line to her destination. There were only villages and small towns through the lowlands, difficult to identify from the air. Her main navigation point was the large Lake Guerrero about twenty-five miles northeast of Victoria. From there she would climb into the real mountains where the city, the rail line or both should be easy to find.

Cruising along at 140 knots Rita made good time. The air was smooth and visibility unlimited. An hour and a half into the flight with the mountains drawing close, Rita began looking ahead and to her left hoping to sight Lake Guerrero. The ground was gradually rising through low rolling hills. Minutes later, Rita caught sight of blue ahead of her as the lake came into view. Soon she was flying directly over it. Immediately Rita banked right onto a heading of 225 degrees. On her new course directly toward the now looming mountains, Rita thought to herself, *Hmmmn, off course slightly to the east.* The only answer was that winds out of the west had pushed her to the east.

The ground was rising as she flew deeper into the higher foothills of the Oriental range. The ground was rockier with narrow valleys and tree covered hillsides. Ahead towered much higher mountains, many near ten thousand feet high, she judged. Gradually Rita let the Vega climb to match the terrain.

A half hour after turning southwest, already into the mountains, Rita flew directly over a railway running almost north south. She was at six thousand feet, now. She judged her height at about three thousand feet above the railway. Gradually the towering mountain range climbed ahead of her. Flying past, she circled back over the rail line trying to decide whether Ciudad Victoria was northwest or southeast along the line. Flipping a mental coin, Rita banked right and followed the rail line south southeast. Ten minutes later, she spotted the capital of Tamaulipas State ahead.

Passing over Ciudad Victoria, Rita followed the rail line as it climbed into the mountains. The pass it was running through climbed steadily. Rita climbed as well, letting the Vega gradually climb to sixty-five hundred feet. The map was too small a scale to show exact altitude of San Rosario but she guessed it was close to four thousand feet. She was now flying over the eastern edge of the rugged Sierra Madre Oriental range. To her left between low peaks she could glimpse the highlands falling away to the distant coastal plain.

Fifteen minutes later the rail line gradually bent until it ran almost due south. Soon after that she spotted a town nestled along the tracks in the mountains ahead. She glanced at her watch. Nearly three o'clock. Throttling back to 125 knots, Rita flew along the tracks which here were paralleled by a road that eventually became a main street through the town. As she flew over the town, she rocked the wings gently back and forth to see downward. She felt through the control wheel the aircraft being jarred by wind. She also noticed she was having to push in a bit of right rudder to keep straight along the center of town. She judged it was more than two thousand feet below her.

Soon she passed it. The town wasn't particularly large but there were some solid looking, multi-story buildings near the center as well as the ever present, large stone cathedral on the town square that seemed to be a fixture in every Mexican city or town. The town was nestled in a valley with small farms scatted around the outskirts. Rita climbed another thousand feet scanning for the airfield.

She soon sighted a long straight slash through trees, a few miles east of town. Banking that way Rita was overhead five minutes later. It wasn't much to look at, Rita decided. There was a single grass runway running almost north-south. Near the southern end several single engine aircraft were lined up to the east of the runway. West of these were two large and one smaller building that appeared to be hangars. Near them were a couple of autos and what looked like a fuel truck.

As Rita banked around for another pass over the field, she could feel the Vega being buffeted by the wind. Coming up from the south, she flew straight up the length of the airstrip. It appeared to be over two thousand feet long by her best guess. Most importantly on this pass she spotted a long red windsock on a tall pole near the south end of the strip. As she climbed away Rita chewed her lower lip. The problem was the wind sock was streaming out to the east. That could be a problem.

With the airstrip oriented more or less north-south any aircraft could make a long approach along the length of the valley. That was all good, but winds out of the west meant a crosswind while landing. Even now she could feel winds buffeting her aircraft. The question was; how much wind was there? There was no control tower to check with for wind speed. She would have to guess and hope for the best.

Rita circled around to the north and gradually bled off speed as she throttled back and let the Vega sink towards the ground. As the aircraft slowed, Rita wished mightily that the Vega had flaps like the Shrikes did. It would make the aircraft more stable at low speed. Her speed was down to 110 now and she judged her altitude at about four hundred feet above the ground. With the nose slightly down Rita had a good view of the strip ahead. She could see her nose swing left and feel the wind vibrating the controls. She dipped her right wing slightly and pushed in right rudder to straighten up. Three hundred feet. She pulled the nose up slightly to kill her speed just as another gust pushed her left. She pushed in hard right rudder and the nose swung back to the right. She was still moving ahead but her nose was now pointed off her course. Two hundred feet now and speed down below a hundred. Rita took a deep breath. This was going to be tricky.

With the nose pointed to the right and the aircraft crabbing forward at an angle, Rita was straining to see the runway ahead past the big engine. More wind hit and she had to lower the right wing even more. With her starboard wing down to keep from being blown to port she could see even less ahead She bit her lip as she crabbed ahead craning her neck up trying for a glimpse of the airstrip. She was now judging her direction from the trees to the west of the strip. Air speed was down to ninety. Eighty-five. She couldn't judge her height exactly but knew she close to the ground. Over the end of the strip another gust hit her ship and threatened to push her eastward.

With her starboard wingtip dangerously close to the ground, Rita yanked back the throttle and pulled gently back, flaring the ship. She leveled her wings and tapped left rudder. Her starboard gear hit first, followed immediately by the port gear. She bounced but pushed the wheel forward and got both wheels down on the ground. She bounced again, less high this time. Then, both main wheels were down. She was out of the wind and running fast down the strip. Rita tapped the left brake pedal to straighten the nose. The Vega's nose came around. The tail dropped and Rita was on the ground.

She pressed hard on both brakes. The Vega slowed and Rita craned upward trying to see over the big Pratt & Whitney engine. Giving up on this, she leaned to her right as much as she could and waited for the hangars to appear in her vision. Slowing still more, she finally saw the hangars appear to the right, she steered that way using brakes and cut the engine as they neared.

The prop swung to a stop and Rita brought the aircraft to halt. She sat for a moment, before blowing out a long breath and sighing, "Any landing you can walk away from . . ." Unbuckling her seat belt she unlatched the overhead hatch. Pushing it back she lifted herself half out of the ship and looked around.

Just ahead were the three buildings. She had brought the Vega to a stop right in front of them. Rita nodded, thinking, *Just like I planned.* One of the larger hangars was closed. Inside the other one she could see a biplane inside with a coveralled mechanic working on the engine. The smaller building seemed to be a combination garage and office. Even now a man was walking from it toward her. He raised a hand and waved. Rita waved back.

Dropping down into the ship she pulled open the seatback/ door to the main cabin and walked down to the cabin door on the right side. She pushed it open and stepped down out of the aircraft. It was windy on the ground as well as in the air. At this altitude it was much cooler than the airfield in Laredo. She guessed the temp as about seventy. Unzipping her leather jacket as the man approached, Rita held up a hand, smiled and said, "*Hola*."

The man wore coveralls and was wiping his hands on a once white towel, "*Buenos Dias, Señorita*."

Rita had taken three years of Spanish in High School but had not had to use it much lately. Her understanding was good but her vocabulary limited. Summoning up her memories, she told the man she was here to meet someone.

He shrugged, "No one here, Señorita."

Rita frowned and said, "An American? Waiting to be flown out?"

He again shrugged, "*Lo siento*, Señorita. Not here today."

Rita looked around. Dave was supposed to be here waiting. Rob said he had sent a telegram…unless Dave hadn't received it. Rita knew that communications in Mexico often were hit or miss. Maybe the telegraph was down. She looked at her watch. It was three-thirty. She had maybe three hours of daylight left. There were no lights on this field and if they didn't get off soon, they would have to wait until tomorrow. Town wasn't far but how to get there?

Turning to the…mechanic? Airfield manager? She wasn't sure. Whoever he was, Rita gave him her best smile and asked if he could tie down her airplane and watch it until she returned. She must go into town to look for her friend.

The man smiled back and replied, "*Si. Gasolina, tambien?*"

Rita shook her head, "No. *Gracias.*" She pulled a wad of Rob's pesos out of her pocket and after some brief haggling the two came to an agreement. As she handed over some money she asked, "How can I get into town?"

The man replied in English, "Taxi. I call."

Rita thanked him and turned for the Vega to gather up her gear. It didn't take long for the taxi to arrive. Fifteen minutes later a battered black Model T sedan rattled onto the airfield. As Rita got in, she saw the field manager and a couple of mechanics pushing the Vega off the field toward the line of parked airplanes. The driver ignored them and immediately accelerated away from the field. Rita started to tell him where to go but quickly realized there probably was no place to go other than town. She sat back trying to find a spot where a spring did not poke into her backside.

While they rattled toward town, Rita had dug out the name of the hotel where Dave was staying. As they wheezed down the dusty road Rita asked in Spanish, "Are you the only taxi in town?"

Keeping his eyes on the road the driver threw over his shoulder in broken English, "No. There are two other taxis here, but you would no want to ride with them." He patted the wheel fondly, "Isabella, she is the best."

Rita smiled to herself, "I'm looking for a friend here. An Americano. He has been here a week. Maybe you know him?"

"What he look like?"

"His name is David Parsons. He is young and tall."

"*Lo siento, señorita*. I not know him."

Rita pulled a five dollar bill out of her pocket and reached it forward next to her driver's shoulder, "Maybe you could ask around and see if your taxi friends know him."

The driver took the bill and nodded vigorously, "Si. I ask. Where we go now?"

Rita leaned back and wiggled uncomfortably, "Hotel Paradiso."

"Si."

Minutes later they entered San Rosario. It wasn't the sleepy Mexican town Rita had expected. There were quite a few people on the streets. Lots of women, many carrying bags or packages. There were shop keepers out on front of their

Rita asked if he could tie down her airplane and watch it...

stores sweeping the wooden sidewalks or men lounging in front of businesses or cantinas. The taxi eventually entered the town square and crossed it carefully, the driver sounding his horn to scatter pedestrians.

The taxi then pulled up in front of a three-story stone and wood building. Rita got out, paid the driver. He thanked her and said, "I be back." Hefting up her briefcase and overnight bag Rita entered the hotel as the taxi wheezed away.

Inside Rita crossed the to the registration desk. The lobby was deserted except for a young boy in a red uniform dozing in a chair and a man in a suit at the desk. As she approached, he sized her up quickly and greeted her in quite good English, "*Buenos Dias, señorita*. What can we do for you today?"

"Buenos Dias. I'm here to meet a friend; David Parson, an American. Is he registered here?

"Si, señorita. Señor Parson is staying here."

Rita was a bit surprised to hear this but kept a neutral face and asked, "Is Señor Parsons in his room?"

The desk clerk turned and looked up at the wall of small pigeon holes marked with room numbers. Many had keys in them. He turned back and said, "Señor Parsons is out, I'm afraid. Would you like to wait for him?"

Rita frowned, "Do you know when he will return?"

"No, señorita. I do not. His key was in its place when I arrived today."

Rita thought this over. Deciding, she asked, "Do you have a room near his?"

"Si."

"Good. I will take that room for the night."

While Rita pulled a wad of pesos out of her pocket, the clerk turned the large registration book around and said, "Please sign here."

He then turned and reached for a key off the wall. Rita set some money on the counter and quickly signed in. The clerk handed her the key and said, "Room 208, second floor." He then rang a bell on the counter. The uniformed bell boy stretched and wandered over, yawning as he did. The clerk told him, "Take the señorita up to room 208."

As the bell boy picked up her bag Rita asked, "Is this near to Señor Parsons room?'

"Si, señorita. Right next door."

Rita was surprised to see that the hotel actually had an elevator when the bell boy led her to it. Inside he closed the door and skillfully operated the handle to raise them to the second floor. Once there he led her down the hall to room 208. Rita pulled out a coin and handed it to the young man but did not let it go as he reached for it. She asked, "Do you know Señor Parsons?"

"The Americano in the next room?" he pointed to the door on the left.

"Si."

The boy shrugged, "He has not been here all day. I saw him yesterday, though."

Rita smiled and let go the money. The boy tipped his hat and hustled away. Thoughtfully, Rita unlocked her door and entered. It was a very ordinary hotel room with a bed, dresser, wardrobe, sink in a corner and a window that looked over the street. She tossed her briefcase and bag on the bed, then walked to the window. Pulling back the sheer curtains she peered down on the square and wondered, "All right, Dave. Where are you?" Knowing what Dave was up to down here, made the possible answers unpleasant.

Frowning she turned and went to her briefcase. Opening the top wide she pulled out charts, manuals, pens, pencils, dividers, her .38 revolver and finally reached the bottom. Moments later she came up triumphantly with some paper clips. Choosing two of the largest, she straightened them out and twisted them together until she had a fairly rigid metal implement nearly three inches long. Moving quietly to the door she pressed her ear against it and listened for a minute. Hearing nothing she quietly opened the door and peered out. The hallway was empty. Closing her door behind her she quickly slipped over to the door of Dave's room.

Rita was not a professional thief. Fortunately, the hotel's locks were old fashioned, warded locks. It still took her a couple of very long, nerve wracking minutes manipulating her makeshift skeleton key, during which she was sure someone would show up and ask what she was doing, before the lock turned. Breathing out a sigh, she opened the door and slipped inside. Only to find that she wasn't the only person who knew how to pick locks.

The room had been hurriedly searched. The wardrobe door stood open. Dave's suitcase was on the bed, open. Clothes were strewn everywhere. All the dresser drawers had been pulled out. Rita looked everything over carefully. There was no blood or signs of a struggle. And nothing seemed damaged or destroyed in the room. If you replaced all the clothes in the suitcases or dresser it would look like nothing had ever happened here. So, someone was looking for something. Someone who was probably a lot better at picking locks than Rita was.

Rita stood thoughtfully looking around. This didn't look good. Where was Dave? On the run? Hiding out somewhere? Maybe hurt? A prisoner? What was somebody looking for? And who were they? Dave was here on a recon mission. If someone had become suspicious enough to search his room, they would have been looking for incriminating evidence of who and what Dave was. He most likely would have been carrying his passport with him; that is if he had been traveling under his own name. But was he? The hotel thought so. Suddenly, Rita wished she had asked Rob for better instructions before she left. All right, what else could the unknown persons be looking for? Dave might have made notes or left a journal of his observations. Or would he? Dave was careful, chances were he would leave little to find or if he did, it was most likely in a private code of some kind.

So, if whoever it was had not already found it, where would it be? Rita turned in a circle. Where hadn't been searched? Dropping to one knee next to the bed she stuck her arm between the thin mattresses and swept it back and forth. She repeated this around the bed but found nothing. Turning she sat and leaned her back against the bed. Brushing a stray lock of her long red hair back from her face, she blew out her breath and stared at the opposite wall. Was there any place that hadn't been searched? Frowning she thought about turning back the rug covering a good bit of the room. That would entail moving furniture around, though.

Rita lifted herself up, brushed off her bottom with one hand and walked over to the sink. Thirsty, she turned the cold water tap and filled the glass sitting on the edge of the porcelain sink. The water was not very cold but tasted fine to Rita after her long day. As she set the empty glass down, it hit her. Dropping quickly to one knee she reached her right hand up and ran it along the inside surface of the porcelain sink. Immediately she felt something hard. She pulled and with a ripping of tape, the something came loose.

It was a small black automatic pistol. Rita pulled off the tape and hefted it. A pound and half she guessed, less than six inches long with a three-inch barrel, the pistol had a large "S" cast into the hard rubber grips. Peering at it carefully, she read the small print engraved into the barrel; *Sauer 7.65mm*. She ejected the magazine and found it fully loaded. So, Dave had stashed his gun here. That meant he had not been expecting trouble whenever he ran into it. Most likely he had been caught unaware.

Rita slipped the little .32 into her pants pocket. Sliding to the door she listened carefully, but hearing nothing she slipped out, leaving the door unlocked behind her. Back in her own room she sat on the edge of the bed staring at Dave's little pistol. How to find him? The best way was probably to follow his last moves. That taxi driver had better come up with some good news.

No sooner than this thought passed her mind than there was a noise in the hall. A moment later came a knock on her door. She stood up quickly, "*Quien es?*"

A heavily accented voice came through the door, "Jose, the taxi."

Rita turned and dropped the little pistol into her briefcase, followed by her revolver. She then walked to the door and opened it. Her driver stood there, hat in hand. He smiled and said, "I find, you know, your friend."

Rita motioned him into the room and closed the door, "Tell me what you know."

He nodded, "Mi friend Carlos, drive taxi also. He know you friend. He find at train station and drive heem around town. Last night he drive heem again. He no see heem since." He smiled proudly.

Rita thought for a moment, her mind racing across possible actions. Finally she smiled, "I need to go shopping. Then you're going to drive me around exactly where your friend drove my friend."

Jose nodded happily.

Two hours later, back in her room, Rita smoothed down the front of her new dress. It was colorful with a wide skirt and full petticoat underneath. Matching heels completed her outfit. Just the thing for a night out flamenco dancing. The thought of her fellow pilots' mouths dropping open at the sight of her made Rita grin.

Turning, she hefted her revolver and Dave's little Sauer. Weighing them up, she reluctantly decided her Smith & Wesson was a bit big for social occasions. She then raised one foot up onto a chair. Pulling up the dress hem she exposed a good bit of shapely calf and thigh. With the medical tape she had purchased at a local drug store near the dress shop she quickly taped the little Sauer to the inside of her left thigh.

Ready, she grabbed her new purse and set off on the night's adventure. Downstairs she left her room key with the desk clerk and told him she would return after dinner. He nodded and smiled as he watched Rita's trim figure cross the lobby to the front door. Outside Jose was waiting in his rickety taxi. He jumped out and held the door for her as she entered.

Inside she said, "First, the cantina."

"Si," Jose replied putting the auto in gear and pulling away from the hotel with a jerk. After making her purchases earlier, Rita had Jose take her around to the places Dave had visited the night before. They did not stop, just cruised by them so Rita could size them up. First on the list had been what she had at first thought was a small, rundown hotel. Jose had quickly informed her differently.

"Is a uh…a um house for uh…for um…*pleasure*." She couldn't see her driver's face from the back seat but she could feel his embarrassment as she realized he was trying to tell her the building was a brothel. Rita felt a bit of warmth in her own cheeks as she said calmly, "I understand."

The next stop was a busy cantina that Jose told her was frequented by many gringos. Rita noted that it was busy as they drove slowly past. Finally, Dave's last stop was a large warehouse in a rundown area north of town. Not far from the railroad tracks. She had ordered Jose not to slow down but to drive past. If Dave was looking for someone he might have gone to the brothel, then the cantina. Finding out what he wanted to know, he had then gone to the warehouse. And, there the trail ran cold. Her best hope was to retrace his steps and see what developed.

For obvious reasons she decided that the cantina would be an easier place to get information than the bordello. At the cantina, Rita gave Jose some money and told him to wait. She entered. The place was loud and busy. It was filled with locals and a surprising number of obvious foreigners. A trio of Mariachi's played loudly from a corner. Rita found a table and watched the crowd while she waited for service.

There were more than half a dozen roughly dressed foreigners at the bar or at tables. Miners from nearby mines, no doubt. There were also three more prosperous men in suits; obvious foreigners from their suits and looks. There were more than a few local girls, colorfully dressed as Rita was, some accompanying men, some laughing and drinking while competing for attention. Eventually a waitress in a colorful skirt and white, low cut peasant blouse made her way through the crowd and took Rita's order for food. When the girl asked what Rita wanted to drink, she hesitated unsure what to order here in Mexico. Then her eye caught one of the suited foreigners at a nearby table. He was pouring salt on the back of his hand that held a section of lemon. In his other hand he held a small glass. Licking the salt off his hand, he quickly threw down the liquid in the glass and bit into the lemon. Rather surprised at this show, Rita looked up at the girl and asked, "What is that?"

The girl laughed and replied, "Mezcal." She turned and disappeared. Rita shrugged and watched the crowd. In return she got many interested looks. Finally one of the suited men came over. He tipped his hat and said in English, "This is not a very good place for ladies," in a vaguely French accent.

Rita smiled, "Do I look that American?"

The Frenchman smiled in return. "You are far too beautiful for San Rosario. Can I take you somewhere more appropriate to your beauty?"

"I'm sorry, but I am waiting for someone. Perhaps you know him? A tall young American?"

The man gave a Gallic shrug, "There are many Americans here. They come and go." He bowed slightly and backed away. Rita's food then arrived. The girl also set down a small glass of amber colored liquid, a salt shaker and a wedge of lemon. Rita had eaten very little that day and dug in with relish. Moments later she needed relief from the spicy food.

She looked at the glass in front of her. Shrugging she poured some salt on the back of her hand. It all ran off onto the table. Frowning, she reluctantly licked the back of her hand and tried again. This time the salt stuck nicely. Picking up the lemon in the salt covered hand, she lifted the glass and sighed, "Here goes." Licking the salt, she quickly downed the glass. The fiery liquid burned as she swallowed. Quickly she bit into the lemon and sighed as the sour fruit juice mixed with the alcohol.

"Whewww!" Rita gasped and shook her head. She licked her salty lips and blew out a breath. That had been something. She could still taste the Mezcal and lemon in her throat. She gave a shake of her head, picked up her fork and went back to her dinner. She kept an eye on the crowd. Although she received many admiring looks no one else approached her. Finished, she considered another drink. She was tempted but reluctantly decided that much more of that Mezcal and the only place she would be going was home to bed. Instead she caught the serving girl's attention and ordered a, *"Cerveza, por favor."*

The girl soon brought the beer and as she leaned in she whispered, "I hear what you say. A young, guapo Americano was here last night. He leave late with an *extranjero*" Rita knew that meant foreigner. She nodded her thanks and sipped her beer. She continued watching as people came and went. The mariachis took a break. Taking advantage of the quiet a man approached her table. Rita sized him up as she sipped. He was Mexican she judged but was wearing a cheap suit rather than working clothes. He was thin and sharp eyed with black hair combed straight back that gleamed with hair oil.

At the edge of the table he eschewed a slight bow and said, "Señorita, I unnerstand you are looking for a gringo friend. A man, American, young, the hair is light?" His English was pretty good although heavily accented.

Rita, nodded, "Si. You know him?"

The man shrugged, "No. But I see him here last night."

"Where did he go?'

Another shrug, "I do not know, but I see heem talk to another man, a business man."

"How can I find this business man?"

The thin man thought for a moment, "I can make ask around. You are here? Or perhaps at your hotel?"

Rita nodded, "I'll wait here."

The thin man smiled and said, "I return soon." Smiling, he left quickly.

He was barely out the door before Rita was on her feet. She tossed a wad of pesos on the table and hustled to the door. She ducked into the shadows of the wooden sidewalk and looked both ways. Thirty yards away the thin man was crossing the street heading north. Glancing around she quickly found Jose`s taxi parked nearby, Jose` asleep behind the wheel. She jumped into the back seat and prodded him awake.

Pointing out her quarry she whispered, "Follow him, lights out. And stay way back. He can't know we're following him."

"Si." Jose pressed the starter and the auto wheezed to life. They waited until the thin man was out of sight and then rolled slowly forward. Leaning over his shoulder to peer through the dusty wind screen, Rita nervously watched ahead. Catching sight of her man in the brief glow from a dim street light, Rita ordered Jose` to slow. Seconds later, she saw the flare of a momentary light and realized the thin man had lit a cigarette. This made their pursuit easier as they could now follow the dim glow of his cigarette as he moved north along the deserted street.

Deciding she could guess her quarry's destination, Rita made a bold move. She ordered Jose, "Turn on your head lights and drive straight to the warehouse you took me to earlier." Ducking down in the back as Jose complied, the taxi rattled past the thin man and moved ahead. After a few turns the taxi pulled up in front of the warehouse minutes later. Pointing, Rita handed over a fist full of pesos and told Jose, "Park a couple of blocks over and wait for me. I may be a while." Nodding, he took the money as she hopped out.

When the taxi had chugged around a corner. Rita took cover around the far corner of the warehouse and waited. Minutes passed and she was beginning to doubt her plan when around a corner came the thin man. He walked up to the warehouse, threw down the butt of his cigarette and banged on a door in the front of the building. Rita took this as her cue to fade away down the narrow alley flanking the warehouse looking for a second entrance. Finding nothing, she continued as far as the back of the warehouse.

This ran along a narrow street. Above Rita's head, dim light showed through some dust covered windows. She quickly found a small door near the corner. It was locked. Rita reached into her purse and felt around. She smiled as her fingers closed on her makeshift lock pick. Remembering her experience earlier in the evening, she had the door unlocked in a little over a minute.

The door only gave off one small squeak as she slipped into the darkened warehouse. Pulling the door closed behind her, Rita turned and immediately bumped into something hard in the near darkness. Using her hands to explore the barrier she found it was made wooden barrels stacked vertically leading away from the door. She followed the along the row, her eyes gradually adjusting to the dim light in the warehouse.

Reaching the end of the row of barrels, she peered around them. This end of the warehouse was filled with stacks of wooden barrels, old packing crates and piles of unidentifiable junk. Ahead of her there was even a good-sized stack of hay bales. Past this Rita could see the soft glow of a light. Carefully she made her way forward.

Inching up to the stack of haybales, Rita peered around the edge. Ahead of her in a pool of light cast by two lanterns, one set on the ground and another hanging from a support beam, two dark-haired, rough-looking locals stood sharing a drink from a bottle. To one side a tall, dark-haired man in a suit with a fedora obscuring his face stood listening to the thin man she had followed from the cantina. Nearest to her, a blonde-haired man sat tied to a chair, his back to her. His head hung forward and he appeared to be unconscious. She could not be sure from the rear but Rita was sure it must be Dave Parsons.

In Spanish, the tall man asked the thin man she had followed, "You're sure the woman was asking about this man." He pointed to a figure bound to a chair.

"Si, Patron`. I am sure. She too was Americano."

"And she's waiting at the cantina?"

"Si."

"All right, we're going back there and get her." He turned to the two ruffians and said, "Watch him. We'll be back soon."

The two turned and disappeared into the darkness. A moment later Rita heard a door slam. *Interesting*, Rita thought. The tall man in the fedora was obviously the leader here. He spoke Spanish but it was not the casual Spanish spoken by most Mexicans. She had heard that accent before; from her High School Spanish teacher who had studied in Europe. He called his accent "Castilian." Just who were these guys?

Various plans ran through Rita's mind. She could hold both these guys at gun point but Dave was unconscious. What she needed was some kind of distraction. Maybe she could exit and lure them away somehow. As she thought, one of the two remaining toughs spoke rapidly to his partner; too fast for Rita to follow. She thought it sounded like he wanted something. His partner replied that he needed to answer a call of nature. The two parted, heading off in different directions. Moments later, Rita heard a door slam.

Knowing a gift when she saw one, Rita quickly made her way into the light and knelt behind Dave's chair. She shook his shoulder and whispered, "Dave! It's Rita. Are you okay?" While she spoke, she was digging in her purse.

Dave lifted his head and groaned, "Uhhhhh…Rita? What the heck are you doing here?"

Still rooting around blindly in her purse, she whispered, "I'm here to rescue you."

Dave shook his head trying to clear it, "Rescue? Rob sent you?"

"Yeah. I seem to be doing a lot of that lately."

"Where is everyone?"

Yes! Rita's hand closed on the object she was desperately searching for, "Two of them took off for the cantina looking for me. The other two are around here somewhere. One was headed for a bathroom. Don't know if it's out in back or what. The other might be back any time." As she whispered these words, Rita was prying open the blade of her small pen knife with a nail. Finding Dave's

"All right, we're going back there and get her."

bound hands in the darkness she began sawing at the rough ropes.

A minute later, with the rope cut most of the way through, one of the toughs stepped into the light. Surprised he called out, "*Quien eres*?" *Who are you?*

Caught, Rita's thoughts raced for a solution. She pressed the pocket knife into Dave's palm and stood up. Stepping away from him and straightening her shoulders, she spoke boldly in English, "This is my fiancé. Why are you holding him here?"

The roughly dressed man seemed at a loss for words. He reached for the gun at his waist and said, "*No te muevas!*" Then raising his voice he yelled, "Pedro!"

Desperate to buy time for Dave, Rita spoke loudly, "We are Americans! You cannot treat us this way!"

Seconds later, the second Mexican tough came running in from somewhere yelling, "*Que` pasa,* Jose?"

The first tough pointed his revolver at Rita and rattled off something that she did not catch. She yelled out, "Help!" hoping to confuse things a bit more. The newly arrived tough seemed surprised. He pointed at Rita and asked his partner who she was. The other one replied and the two argued for a minute over who she was and what to do.

Rita glanced to the side. Dave was unmoving. She knew he was awake but had he freed himself yet? The other two men would soon return. They had to make their move quickly.

A minute later, she heard voices from somewhere in the warehouse. *Uh oh,* Rita thought. *That sounded like…It was.* The tall man strode into the light, the thin Mexican trailing behind him.

The thin man pointed. "That is her, Patron`."

Rita glanced around. It didn't look good. Both toughs now had pulled revolvers and pointed them loosely at Dave and Rita. Dave raised his head and looked blurrily around. She could see why. He had been badly beaten. His jaw was heavily bruised and one eye was swollen nearly shut. Dried blood trailed down his face and neck and was splashed all over his once white shirt.

The tall man spoke to Rita in cultured English, "You know this man?"

"Yes. He is my fiancé. I came here to meet him."

The tall man pushed his fedora back a bit and Rita saw his face clearly for the first time. He did not have the sunburned, dark complexion of a native to this part of the country. He had fine features with dark hair and a pencil thin mustache. Intelligent dark eyes evaluated her. Not changing his expression or gaze, he spoke one word, "Buscala!"

The thin man stepped forward to search Rita. He grabbed her purse from her hand. She yelled, "Hey!" Rummaging through it he shook his head and tossed it down. Grabbing Rita's shoulder he spun her around, his hand running along the waist of her skirt. He then reached for the hem of her dress to pull it up. This was her cue. Rita turned and slapped the thin man in the face, putting as much strength into it as she could muster while shouting, "How dare you!"

The blow caught him square on the cheek and he staggered back two steps, his hand to his cheek. Things happened quickly then. Both toughs laughed loudly at the associate's embarrassment. The thin man's face darkened and he stepped toward Rita, his hands now fists. He swore at the same time the tall man told him to calm down in Spanish. Dave, his hands now free, chose this moment to launch himself out of his chair at one of the toughs. His shoulder hit the man square in the chest and Dave and he went down together in a heap. The thin man in front of her froze, surprised by Dave's move. Rita shoved him in the chest with both hands sending him staggering back into the tall man. She then dodged back toward the shadows.

Ducking down behind a stack of boxes, Rita clawed under her skirt. Dave's little pistol came loose with a strong pull, along with the length of medical tape ripping along her tender thigh. Leaning around the side of the crate, she thumbed off the safety and pointed it at the thin man who had pulled a pistol from under his jacket. Bang! Rita squeezed the trigger and saw the thin man stagger. He grabbed his side and staggered backwards firing at Rita as he sought cover. A bullet whizzed over her head. Another one smacked into the crate she was crouched behind. Yells in Spanish were drowned out by more shots.

Somewhere in the darkness a voice called out in Spanish, "Kill them!"

Rita could hear curses and grunts from the two men struggling on the floor. She ducked again at the flash of a gun that was fired at her from the shadows. Once more came the angry buzz of a slug flashing past her head. She could hear but not see the sounds of men struggling. She called out, "Dave, are you okay?" As she did, she realized how stupid it sounded.

Angry, Rita raised her weapon. Just as she squeezed the trigger an incoming bullet hit the crate next to her. A splinter tore into the back of her hand. Jerking the gun downward her bullet hit the lantern sitting on the ground. It shattered immediately spreading a three-foot wide pool of burning kerosene across the floor. In the glare of the burning liquid Rita could see the tall man across the warehouse. He was waving a pistol and shouting, "Put out the fire!"

Rita stood up to take aim at him. It was a long shot for the little pistol but she raised the weapon and took a breath and fired. The smack of a fist on flesh came from her right. The Mexican tough Dave had been fighting staggered into the light and fell on his back, arms wide, out cold. She looked at him in surprise as Dave staggered up to her, "Are you all right?"

Rita ducked as an incoming bullet buzzing past. She yelled out, "Just peachy! How 'bout you?"

Dave tried to wipe blood from his face as he gasped out, “Rita! We gotta go!”

She nodded, “Right behind you. The door’s back there.” She pointed into the dark the way she had come. Dave turned and limped off. She looked back the other Mexican tough had scrounged up a blanket and was beating at the flames. She couldn’t see the tall man but she could see her purse lying on the floor ten feet away. Biting her lip Rita lunged forward. She hit the floor on her knees. She grabbed the purse, fired twice at the surprised man with the blanket. He staggered back and dropped the now burning blanket. It fell amongst loose straw on the ground. Rita rolled back toward the crates.

Getting to her feet Rita ran toward the back corner of the warehouse. It was dark, she tripped once and barked her shins twice before finally reaching the now open back door. In the relatively bright light of the alley she found Dave leaning against a wall.

Looking back, Rita could see smoke wafting out the open door. The fire would probably spread. She shook her head…*not good.* She felt a hand on her arm and Dave wheezed, “Rita, we gotta get outta here now!”

“Sure, Dave. I got a taxi waiting a couple of blocks over.”

“No! You don’t understand. That warehouse has a ton of weapons and explosives inside. We gotta get outta here before it blows!”

“Then let’s go!” Rita grabbed him by the arm and pulled him down the alley. At the corner she turned the wrong way. The dark streets and alleys all looked the same. By the time she found the taxi, Jose, again asleep behind the wheel, they could see the glow of the fire over a nearby building. They piled into the car as the first explosion lit the sky behind them.

Moments later as the now wide awake Jose navigated the narrow streets, Rita asked Dave, “How bad are you hurt?”

He groaned, “I feel like a carpet out on the clothes line being beaten. Where are we going?”

“Back to the hotel. We gotta get our things and get out of here”

Dave winced as he nodded, “Did you fly down?”

“Yep. In the Vega. It’s out at the airfield now.”

Dave nodded, “Good.” He closed his eyes and leaned his head back against the battered leather seat. As they neared the town square a local fire engine raced past them. Clinging to it were half dressed men in wide, leather fire hats. An overweight man in his tee shirt sat in the open next to the driver pulling on a long cord that rang an overhead brass bell. It passed them as Jose politely pulled over. Racing around a corner the old-fashioned rig leaned precariously. So much so that one of the firemen struggling into his heavy coat was nearly thrown off the fire truck. Only by clinging to one of the long vertical handrails did he manage to hang on with this fellow fire fighters frantically grabbing at him. Rita's mouth dropped open. It reminded her of a Mack Sennett comedy with the Keystone Cops.

Moments later, they pulled up in front of their hotel. Rita told Jose, "Keep the motor running." Jumping out, she told Dave, "Hang on. I'll just be minute."

He grabbed her hand, "You know this is the first place they'll look for us."

"I know but all the charts and maps are up there, not to mention my gun. I won't be long, trust me." She smiled before stepping into the sleepy hotel. The lobby was empty at this time of night. The desk clerk was dozing on a stool behind the counter. The bell boy was asleep on a sofa. Rita hustled quietly up the stairs.

Seconds later she stood in front of her door. Pulling her makeshift skeleton key from her purse, she was inside closing the door behind her a minute later. Quickly changing into her flying gear, she stuffed the dress into her bag and packed her maps and revolver into her briefcase. A bag in each hand she made her way next door to Dave's room. Gathering his clothes together she stuffed them hurriedly into his suitcase and closed it up. Her arms now full, Rita made her way quickly down the stairs.

She plopped her bags noisily on the floor and banged her hand down on the small desk bell. The clerk woke with a start, nearly falling off his stool. Rita smiled at the man wiping sleep out of his eyes, "Checking out, please."

"Uh, Si señorita."

"Also, add Señor Parson's bill on to mine."

The clerk looked surprised but nodded. The bill was quickly figured and Rita handed over some bills. She nodded, "Gracias," gathered up the baggage and hustled out the door.

Back in the taxi, she told Jose, Take us to the airfield."

Jose smiled over his shoulder and shoved the old auto into gear. With a jerk they started off across the darkened square. Rita barely breathed at they wheezed their way through town. At every intersection she expected to be intercepted by enemies. She did not relax her grip on Dave's little pistol concealed in her purse until they reached the road out of town leading to the airfield.

Fifteen minutes later they reached the darkened airfield. Rita directed Jose toward the line of shadowy parked aircraft. As his headlight—only one seemed to be working—swept across the white form of the Vega she said, "*Ese!*" He obediently pulled up next to the aircraft. Rita helped Dave out of the back seat and then piled the bags next to him. Turning, she pulled out a wad of money and handed some to Jose` saying, "You've been a great help, Jose. Gracias."

Taking the money Jose lifted his straw hat briefly and bowed slightly, "Gracias, Señorita."

Hopping back into his battered auto he rattled away, tooting the little bulb horn mounted on the driver's door. Dave shook his head and croaked out, "Where did you find that character?"

Rita handed Dave her briefcase and picked up the other two bags, "You shouldn't judge. I wouldn't have found you without his help."

Rounding the tail of the Vega, Rita opened up the cabin door. Behind her Dave asked, "How did you find me?"

Climbing up into the Vega, she turned and took their bags from Dave, "Had Jose there question his taxi buddies until he found the one who drove you around yesterday. Went to the same places you did and asked around. Sure enough that skinny yahoo at the warehouse came around asking me a lot of questions. I followed him back to the warehouse and voila, rescue."

Dave reached a hand up to her saying incredulously, "You call that a rescue!"

Rita pulled and helped Dave into the cabin. "Maybe I should have left you for the next rescuer. You all seemed to be getting along so well back at the warehouse."

Dave just grunted. Rita pulled a flashlight from its mount on the cabin wall and flipped it on. She helped Dave to one of the passenger seats. "Close your eyes." He obliged and she shined the light on is face. It was not a pretty sight. Shaking her head she gently touched his face in a couple of places, "Can you see out of the left eye at all?"

"Not really. I'm afraid you're going to have to fly us out."

"Well, I got in, I can get us out. Although the winds were pretty nasty when I flew in today."

"I guess Rob got my telegram?"

"Yep. He sent me off this morning. I expected you here at the field. When you didn't show I went looking. Here, let me get some water."

Using the flashlight Rita located a canteen of water in the cockpit and brought it back. She handed it to Dave and he drank deeply, water running down the side of his face. When he lowered it and handed it back. "Thanks, I needed that."

Pulling a handkerchief from her purse, Rita wet it and gently began cleaning the blood from Dave's face. As she did, she asked, "How did they get on to you?"

Wincing, Dave replied slowly, "They didn't or at least they weren't sure. Somehow, they got the word that I was nosing around town asking questions. That's what they were asking me all day. Who I was and why was I so nosy."

"Well, I guess you didn't tell them much."

"Yeahhh?"

Rita shrugged, "If you had they wouldn't have kept beating on you."

Dave just grunted in reply. Finished, Rita shook her head. "I should have left the blood on your face. It just looks worse now."

Dave said dryly, “Thanks.” Rita took this opportunity to wipe the dried blood from the back of her hand. The wooden splinter had gouged a two-inch long tear into the back of her gun hand. It wasn’t deep and was no longer bleeding.

Rita stood up and made for the cabin door. Dave asked, Where you going?”

“Out to get the chocks and tie downs clear.”

“You know we can’t take off in the dark.”

“I know. But we need to be ready to go as soon as we can.” Rita dropped to the ground. In seconds she had kicked the heavy wood chocks away from the landing gear. Two minutes later the tie downs were loose. In the dark she walked around checking what she could. The rudder, elevators and ailerons all moved freely. The tires felt hard when she kicked them. Other than that she couldn’t do much of a pre-flight inspection.

Back in the cabin she found Dave leaning back in a seat, his eyes closed. He asked, “What time is it?”

In the light of the flashlight Rita looked at her watch, “Just after one.”

Dave opened his eye. “They’ll figure out where we have to be sooner or later.”

Rita nodded solemnly, “Yeah. But I figure if any of those jerks made it out of the fire, they’ll take a while to get organized.”

Dave thought about this for a moment. “I saw skinny guy get it and you got at least one of the tough guys that were beating on me. What happened to the tall guy in the Fedora?

“Don’t know for sure. He was firing from the shadows. Was he the head guy?”

“Yeah. He was European. Maybe Spanish or Italian. He was the one asking the questions. Say! Was that my *Sauer* you were using?”

“Yep. Found it taped under your wash basin. I figured it would be easier to hide than my .38. She pulled the little gun out of her purse and handed it over to Dave.

He took it. “Empty, I suppose.”

“Might have a round or two left. And, give me back my pocket knife. I’ve had that since I was a kid.”

Dave snorted. He gingerly pulled the little knife from his pocket and held it out. As Rita reached for it, he said quietly, “Thanks, Rita. For a while there, I didn’t think I was going to make it.”

Rita took her knife and smiled back, saying lightly, “All part of our regularly scheduled service, sir. I’m sorry our flight will be a little delayed this morning but we’ll be off before you know it.”

Rita picked up her briefcase and moved forward to the cockpit. There she checked her gauges and looked around. Everything seemed normal. Using the flashlight she pulled out her maps and began plotting a course home. Fifteen minutes later she moved back down the cabin to Dave. She plopped down in a seat. "Twenty minutes at 030 should get us down out of the mountains. Then its 345 degrees and home to Laredo."

Dave just nodded. Rita checked the time with the flashlight. Sunrise was sometime before six. It might be light enough for takeoff an hour before. Three hours to wait. She sat silently for several moments before asking, "How much time do you think we have?"

Dave sighed. "Fedora no doubt has other people around. Once he gets them rounded up, they'll try the train depot then the hotels. They'll tell him at the hotel about the taxi. He'll go and roust your friend out. That is, if he doesn't think of the airfield and come straight here."

Rita swallowed, her mouth a little dry. She cleared her throat and asked, "Can you tell me what you found or is that classified?"

"Is there any more water left?" Rita handed him the canteen. After he had a drank, he said, "I came in a week ago. I figured whoever was doing the smuggling was using the railroad from Tampico. Sure enough, I found a lot of stuff was being unloaded here in town at odd times, usually late at night. I started asking around, and somebody got wind of it who shouldn't."

"So what's it all about? Who's behind it?"

"The weapons are all coming off ships from Europe mooring in Tampico. They're being shipped up the railroad and pulled off here. Probably go by truck on back roads from here to the border. It's got all the earmarks of a *Viper* operation."

Rita shook her head, "Turn over a rock and who will you find?"

"Yep," Dave closed his eyes. Rita opened up her bag and rooted around in it. Coming up with her revolver she held it out to Dave, butt first, "Here, take this."

Dave took the gun and frowned, "What's this for?"

"Unwanted company. I'm going to look around." With this she moved aft to the open door and dropped out onto the ground. Rounding the tail Rita walked forward until she stood on the edge of the grass runway. She looked around slowly. It was very dark on the little field. Overhead the sky was clear with a thousand stars brightening the dark sky. All was quiet. A light wind was blowing. She licked a finger and held it up. As usual, it felt cool whichever way she turned it. Grumbling under her breath, she walked across the airfield. Reaching the wind sock she looked up the pole. The sock was stretched out and flapped lazily across the grass strip. A light crosswind she estimated.

Walking back towards the Vega, Rita stopped in the middle of the grass strip and faced down the length of it. The large trees that grew to either side were just darker shadows. She knew they were tall. The breeze against her left cheek told her that with no reference to keep the nose straight they could easily be pushed into those trees. If only she had more light! It wouldn't take much; even a lantern hung in a tree at the end of the strip would do it…if she had a lantern.

Rita trudged back to the plane. She climbed aboard. She moved forward quietly and settled into a seat across from the sleeping Dave. She settled back to wait, trusting to Dave's snoring to keep her awake.

Rita jerked awake. The dark inside of the *Vega* was silent except for the uneven breathing of Dave through his broken nose. She could make out the windows and open door of the airplane in the dim cabin light. How long had she been asleep? Rita got up and moved back to the door. Dropping to the ground she crouched and looked carefully around under the wings and past the nose of the plane. There was no light or movement. Using the flashlight she had grabbed up, she chanced a quick flash on her wristwatch. It was just after four o'clock.

As Rita climbed back into the aircraft, Dave stirred and spoke from the darkness, "Everything okay?"

"Yep." All quiet."

"What time is it?"

"A little after four."

Dave answered with a grunt, "Uhh. Too early for take-off."

Rita shook her head, realized he couldn't see it and said. "Another hour maybe. We should have enough light by then, even before sun up." She worked her way forward saying, "I'm going to run up the engine. When we go, I want it warmed up." Once she passed, Dave stood up to go the other way, toward the cabin door. She frowned, "Where you going?"

Dave climbed down carefully and said, "Uhhh…call of nature." He then disappeared into the darkness. Rita shrugged. She climbed into the cockpit and closed the cockpit door behind her. Reaching for switches from memory she found the master switch and flipped it on. Her gauges lit up. Quickly she adjusted the setting of her controls for start-up and hit the starter switch. The cold engine coughed, misfired, coughed again and finally settled into a rough idle. Rita adjusted the fuel mixture and throttle. Seconds later the engine smoothed out. She scanned the gauges: oil pressure good, cylinder head temperature climbing to normal, oil temp warming.

Rita felt the aircraft shift as Dave climbed back aboard. With the door/seat-back in position she couldn't easily talk to him. She reached to her right and slid open a small window to the passenger compartment, "Dave?"

"Yeah. How's she look?"

"Uhh. Too early for take-off."

"Everything's in the green. Plenty of fuel. We should have an easy trip home."

"Good. I've seen enough of this country for a while!"

Rita smiled. She let the engine run for a few more minutes before shutting it down. Although she left all the settings in takeoff position. Opening the cockpit door she moved back to Dave where he asked, "What's the time?" She picked up the flashlight and checked her watch, "Nearly four thirty."

Dave grunted as Rita moved past him and dropped out of the plane. He was going to ask where she was going but then nodded to himself and relaxed.

Five minutes later Rita was back at the plane. She looked at the sky hoping for the distant light of pre-dawn but knew it was too early. As she turned to climb aboard, a distant droning came to her ears. Engines! Aircraft? Her eyes lifted to the western skyline. Beyond the hangars reflected light could be seen on the tall trees to the west. Headlights!

She climbed into the *Vega* and said "We've got company!"

"What? Where?"

"Cars. Multiple, coming this way, fast!"

Dave stood up quickly, bumping into Rita who was making her way forward. He asked, "Do you have any extra rounds for your revolver?"

"Yes, in my bag," Rita called out over her shoulder as he climbed through the opening into the cockpit. "But we can't shoot it out with them, Dave. They'll have us outgunned. And one round in the wrong place will disable this plane or send it up in flames. We have to go now!"

"Rita! There's not enough light!"

"I know. I'm going use the landing lights to steer by. But I don't have much vision to the side or front. I need you on the starboard side. Watch out the right and let me know if we're getting to close to the trees."

Dave nodded in the darkness, "All right. I don't like it, but you're right. We gotta chance it."

"Good. Close that door and stay quiet. I'll wait as long as I can before starting up."

Rita got the cockpit door closed. She half stood up so she could see over the nose. Keeping her head low until she could barely see over the nose, she could see the hangars to her left across the grass strip silhouctted by the now bright light behind them. She felt the aircraft shift and heard Dave's whisper behind her, "Door's closed what's happening?"

Rita watched two sedans drive around the side of the hangars and slow. She whispered, "Two cars. Can't tell how many men but probably a bunch. They're stopped, just looking around." She watched for several more seconds before adding, "They can see all the aircraft but nothing's moving."

"Maybe they'll get out and take a closer look; give us a shot at them."

"Maybe. No, wait! It looks like they're driving around the hangars." As she watched, the cars drove slowly around the front of the hangars and out of her sight. "Now's our chance! Hang on!"

Rita sat down and quickly pulled her seat belt on tightly. She pressed the starter button and immediately the engine fired up and settled into a steady roar. She reached out and flipped a switch. Instantly the large lights mounted in each wing lit up. She called out, "Here we go!" and shoved the throttle forward. The *Vega* rolled forward. Ten yards out, Rita stood on the right brake. It locked and the engine pulled the nose of the aircraft around. When she thought it had gone ninety degrees, she let off the brake and pushed the throttle all the way forward. The engine wound up to a scream and they rolled down the strip.

Dave had thrown himself across the cabin and pressed his face against a window. He saw two cars roar around the end of the hangars. Headlights glared their way. He yelled out, "Here they come!" He then lunged back to the starboard side as the plane rocked forward faster.

Rita's hands were sweating as she gasped the wheel. She couldn't see anything. To each side was darkness. No matter how much she craned her neck, she couldn't see anything past the looming engine. Then Dave's voice came from the right behind her, "Go left! You're drifting!" Rita tapped the left brake to bring the nose back on track. A glance told her speed was up to fifty knots. She felt something hit the fuselage sharply. Before she could call out; Dave yelled, "They're shooting at us!"

Rita shoved on the already firewalled throttle and swore under her breath. The speed was nearing sixty knots. Dave called out, "A little right, I think." Rita obligingly tapped the right brake, hoping Dave could see something out the side window. Dave for his part could only see reflected light off the ground from the powerful landing lights. All he really had was an impression of the wall of trees to their right.

Another something hit the aircraft. Rita crossed her fingers hoping that whoever was shooting did not hit something critical. She would have been more worried if she could have seen the two autos racing down the airstrip to their left, fire coming from guns pointed out the side windows. Fortunately, their speed was now above seventy knots and it was hard to shoot accurately jouncing around at that speed.

At seventy-five knots, Rita tapped the brakes lightly and pushed the wheel gently forward. This brought up the tail and she could see a bit ahead. Not that darkness was reassuring but she could see her landing lights spreading ahead of her and saw she was again drifting right. She pushed in left rudder and it was catching just enough air to straighten them. At eighty knots Rita could feel the controls firming up as they caught the airflow. She also felt more vibrations as bullets struck the airframe. At eighty-five knots she felt the *Vega* lift off the ground slightly and the ride smoothed out.

Rita resisted the overwhelming urge to pull back on the wheel. She could feel the trees rushing at her but she desperately needed more speed. "C'mon, C'mon!" she whispered as the speed crept up to ninety-five knots. They were off the ground but at no more than thirty feet when the landing lights picked up the trees at the end of the strip. Rita bit her lip and pulled back very gently on the wheel. The wall of green rushed at them. With the speedometer notching 100 knots Rita pulled back again and the Vega lifted gracefully. As they skimmed over the tree tops, something hit the bottom of the aircraft with a bang. Startled, Rita yelled, "What was that?"

Dave's voice came through the window shakily, "I think we clipped some tree tops."

"Oh." Rita shook her head and scanned the instruments. Everything seemed in the green. The engine sounded solid. She let the Vega climb naturally and called over her shoulder, "Do you see any damage back there?"

A moment later Dave's voice came from just behind her shoulder. "There's a couple of holes in the cabin but nothing large; just some air whistling through. Rita glanced right and by the light of the instruments could just make out Dave's face peering through the small window. She gave him a thumb's up.

"I guess we made it. Next stop Texas." She could see his smile even in the dim light

They were headed roughly North Northwest, about 325 degrees. Rita banked to port and let the Vega climb into a wide turn. As she came around to the east at about five thousand feet, she could see lightening along the eastern horizon. She peered at her watch in the dim cockpit light. Almost five o'clock. She leveled out at five thousand feet on a heading northeast. A few minutes later Dave stuck his face through the window and asked, "Do you actually know where we are?"

Rita frowned. "Not exactly. I can't see any landmarks in the dark. But we're headed out of the mountains. Somewhere ahead is Lake Guerrero. That should show up well even before sunrise. That's our check point. From there it's a straight run home to Texas. As she spoke, she realized that she should be sighting the lake soon. "Check out the side windows. Can you see the Lake?"

Two minutes later Dave was back, "Nothing. The ground is still dark below." Rita nodded. It was after just five o'clock. Here at over five thousand feet it was rapidly lightening. Deciding she was too far south, Rita rolled into a left bank, bringing the Vega's nose around to the north. Minutes later she caught sight of a large flat dark area ahead; Lake Guerero. Nosing down she lost altitude while adjusting her heading to fly directly over the center of the lake. Over her shoulder she spoke, "That's it. Coming around to 345 degrees. Next stop Laredo."

Dave replied, "Good. I've had enough of Mexico to last me."

On their new heading at four thousand feet, Rita began to relax. They had made it. It had been a close thing but they had got out in one piece. The sun lifted over the horizon in burst of glorious sunlight. She leaned back and watched the rising sun bathing the lowlands below in warm light. She was imagining how good a hot bath would feel when she was jerked back to reality by Dave, "Rita, there's a plane coming up fast to starboard."

Rita craned her head up an around to the right but could see nothing. "I don't see him. What kind of plane is it?"

"He's coming in fast from four o'clock. Single engine. Not sure what type." There was a slight hesitation then he added, "He's coming right at us."

Rita sat up straight. They were cruising at 140 knots. "How close is he?"

"Uh, maybe a thousand yards or more and closing."

Rita shoved the throttle all the way in. The engine noise increased as they gathered speed. Can you make him out, yet?"

"It's a biplane. Short lower wings, in-line engine, spatted wheels; I think it's military."

"Mexican Air Force?"

"I don't think the Mexicans have anything fast enough to catch us. What's our airspeed?"

"We're doing nearly 170 knots. Full out."

There was a pause, then Dave said, "This guy is faster than us. He's closing up to starboard, I think to get a look at us."

Rita dipped the starboard wing. There, slightly behind was the bandit. It was a sesquiplane as Dave had said. It was painted a light grey below with green and beige camouflage above. She could see the pilot in its open cockpit. He wore a leather flying helmet and goggles above his leather flying jacket. He looked them over for a moment before dropping back.

Dave's voice came to her, "Uh, Rita? That's a Fiat CR-32. We've got trouble!"

Rita gritted her teeth, "Is it armed?"

"Oh yeah! Twin nose guns, probably fifty calibers. He's coming up behind us! Go! Go!"

Rita immediately pushed the wheel far forward as she yelled, "Hang on!"

As she threw the Vega into a steep dive, bright lights twinkled from the bandit's nose. Tracers lanced out into space where the Vega had been a moment before. Dave, his nose pressed against a side window, shouted, "He's shooting!"

The Vega's altimeter unwound rapidly, the hands spinning backwards. They were passing three thousand feet when she saw tracers flash past the nose. Keeping the wings level, Rita kicked in left rudder followed immediately by right rudder, jinking the Vega left and right to keep it out of the bandit's fire.

The Fiat was firing short bursts from a hundred yards behind the diving aircraft. The Vega skidded and twisted away from the Fiat's fire. Frustrated, the enemy pilot put on speed and closed to fifty yards. Dave was glued to the window. "He closing in! Do something, Rita!"

Rita quickly pulled the wheel back to her stomach and spun it to the right. Immediately the nose came up and the right wing dropped. The nose dropped and inverted the Vega fell into a vertical dive. The altimeter spun backwards in a blur. Their speed increased as their altitude fell; two thousand feet, 1500 feet, a thousand. Caught unaware, Dave was thrown against the forward bulkhead. His head banged against it stunning him momentarily.

Caught off guard, the Fiat threw itself after the Vega. Rita had gained a precious few seconds. She watched the altimeter carefully, past it she could see the lowlands growing larger through the wind screen. When it reached 1000 feet, she pulled the throttle back and pulled the wheel back to her stomach. Pulling back with all her strength Rita felt the sweat on her forehead as her vision began to blur from the terrific centrifugal force. Slowly the nose came up. The ground was rushing at them as the nose of the Vega rose at a snail's pace. At less than two hundred feet the Vega finally leveled off, skimming above lowland scenery.

Back under control Rita called over her shoulder, "Dave! Are you okay?" There was no answer, frightened Rita yelled louder, "Dave! Can you hear me? Are you all right?"

Finally there was a groan over Rita's shoulder followed by Dave's shaky voice. "Are you trying to kill us?"

Relieved, Rita shook her head, "Sorry, but I had to shake that guy. Are you okay?"

"Uhhhh, banged my head but I'm all right."

"What happened to the other guy?"

"Wait one." She felt the aircraft shift slightly, then heard Dave said, "He's back there. Maybe five hundred yards and closing!"

Rita swore, "Damn! What's it take to lose this guy?" She craned her head left and right. They were over the lowlands now. Flying over mostly open country, lots of open fields, farms and the occasional low hill or large tree. Nowhere to hide.

Behind her Dave warned, "Break left!"

Mindful of her altitude Rita kept the wings level and pushed in the left rudder all she could. The Vega skidded flat to the left as tracers flashed through the space they had just occupied. She immediately pushed in right rudder and skidded the other way. Knowing this couldn't last, Rita pushed the nose forward. As it dropped, she glimpsed buildings to the right. The altimeter spun backward.

Leveling off at less than a hundred feet. Rita banked gently right and lined up on the farm she had sighted. Ahead there was a low farmhouse, surrounded by small outbuildings and trees. Beyond was large barn. Suddenly Dave screamed, "He's firing!" She felt the Vega vibrate as bullets thudded into the fuselage and wings. Cursing she pushed the nose down even more. Skimming just above a field of tall, green corn the Vega roared past the farmhouse. Wash hanging on a clothes line were blown everywhere. Rita caught a glimpse of running forms and scattering animals as the barn loomed in front of her. Deciding instantly, she banked hard right and two seconds later reversed her bank to the left.

Whipping around the barn, the Vega's port wing barely thirty feet above the ground, Rita hoped this maneuver would force the bandit to climb away for another pass. This hope was crushed as Dave reported, "Wow! He just made it over that barn! I think he scraped his wheels on it!"

Rita was running out of tricks. The bandit would be on her again in seconds. Then she saw out to the right an irregular, wavering line of trees. Some were quite large. There were no rivers hereabouts so that meant they had to be growing along a...She banked toward them. Seconds later she flashed over a wide shallow arroyo. She banked downward to follow its course just as the Fiat once again opened fire.

The dried river bed was free of any obstacles but small saplings and brush. Wheels skimming along the sandy soil, Rita figured they were almost below ground level as the arroyos banks were mostly above her. The Fiat caught unaware by the sudden turn into the arroyo was forced to loop up and around before he could continue the pursuit down the dry riverbed.

Rita knew the time she had bought was fleeting. Sooner or later she would be forced to climb and the faster aircraft would be right there. She called over her shoulder, "Where is he?"

"Still behind us and closing in again."

Rita ground her teeth together. She was out of tricks. Then she saw it. Ahead on the right, above on the bank of the arroyo was a huge oak tree. Towering more than eighty feet high its immense limbs spread at least that far. They were nearly abreast of it when Rita yelled, "Hang on!"

She threw the wheel hard over and skimmed toward the right bank, the oak towering over it. At the last second, she lifted the nose of the Vega and the aircraft popped up out of the arroyo. She immediately kicked in the left rudder skidding the nose to the left and then banked hard right. The right wing tipped less than ten feet off the ground. Rita banked the Vega hard around the left side of the tree, limbs brushing against the upper side of the wing. Past it she leveled the wings and pointed the nose north again.

Seconds passed as Rita kept the Vega headed north as low as she dared fly, lifting gently over small trees. Ahead she could see green and what looked like a building. She called out, “Where is he, Dave?”

Dave answered, “I can’t see him!”

“Where’d he go?”

Moments later Dave’s voice came at her shoulder, “I’m not sure. I don’t see him.” There was a pause, “Maybe he went into the tree…or maybe you scared him off. You sure scared me out of year’s growth!

Rita shook her head, “Yeah. Well, maybe he just wasn’t as desperate as I was.”

She scanned her gauges. “Keep an eye out for him. He might not have given up.” Ahead a farm loomed. Rita pulled the Vega up and skimmed over a windmill. She could see people in the farm yard scattering as the aircraft roared past. Past the farm, Rita gradually climbed to a hundred feet. At least there she wasn’t likely to hit any trees or wandering cows. She let out a long breath and wiped her face. Minutes later with no more signs of pursuit, Rita let the Vega gradually climb upwards. At a thousand feet she got them back on course. Texas was a hundred miles away. Laredo less than two hundred. She scanned her instruments and settled back. They might just make it…if nothing else happened.

“And you’re sure it wasn’t Mexican Air Force,” asked Rob?

Before Rita could answer, Dave lifted the icepack off his face. “Not unless the Mexicans are flying Fiat CR-32s. And, I know they’re not.”

Rita shrugged, “I never got a look at him, Rob. I was too busy dodging trees and barns.”

Rob frowned, “Whoever’s behind the gun smuggling probably called ahead from *San Rosario*.”

“And we know who it has to be,” Dave put in as he leaned back in the chair and pressed the ice bag back against his face.

Rita rubbed her face with a tired hand, “If it wasn’t Viper, who else could it be?”

Rob looked thoughtful, “You’re both probably right. It means the smuggling is a lot more serious than we thought.” He turned as a mechanic appeared in the doorway, “The car is ready, Rob.”

“Good.” He gently took Dave’s arm and lifted him upright, “Let’s get you to the doctor.”

“I just need some rest,” protested the pilot.

“Maybe. But it can’t hurt to have Doc check you out.”

Rita stood up, "I'm going along to keep an eye on him."

Rob nodded. As Dave was helped out the door, he put a hand on Rita's arm. She stopped and looked at him. With the smallest of smiles, Rob shook his head and said, "You, know, Rita, you can turn the simplest jobs into a big adventure."

Rita looked surprised. "This was not my fault, Rob. Things just happened when I got there." She said defensively.

"I know. Get Dave looked after and then you better get some rest too."

Rita nodded as she followed Dave out the door. Rob looked thoughtfully after her, thinking of the report he was going to have to write up for Ron to read.

THE END

The Lockheed Vega is an American five- to seven-seat high-wing monoplane airliner built by the Lockheed Corporation starting in 1927. It became famous for its use by a number of record-breaking pilots who were attracted to its high speed and long range. Amelia Earhart became the first woman to fly solo across the Atlantic Ocean in one, and Wiley Post used his to prove the existence of the jet stream after flying around the world twice.

Rita Returns

If you're reading this, I'm guessing you've already read *Radio Rita vol. 1* and liked it. I get that. There's a lot to like. It's a wonderful book. Great cover, great stories and maybe the best interior art ever done by Airship 27.

If you haven't read volume 1 go and find it. You don't have to read it before you read this but you will definitely want to. Why? See above. I had the honor of writing a story for the first volume and had a blast doing it. The story I wrote ("Frequency") quickly became a personal favorite. I had so much fun with Rita as a character that when Ron Fortier put out calls for more Rita stories, I was first in line.

For those not aware, the parameters for Radio Rita stories were wide open. We could pretty much make it up as we went along with only the most basic of descriptions. This made it simple. My concept of Rita's background and personality were easy. The idea of where she was and what she was up to was a little harder.

Years ago, I discovered the Air Pulps. Not just G-8; those quasi-horror flying pulps were fun but not purely air oriented. There were actually a lot of other pure Air Pulps as well, and I went through a phase of reading any I could get my hands on. I was so taken with them I came up with the idea of a couple of pilots running a for-hire, vagabond air operation around the Caribbean combatting spies, smugglers and pirates. I fleshed this out and it sounded like a lot of fun but alas, I had no place for stories like that at the time.

Flash forward to 2022; Radio Rita comes out of nowhere. So, I dusted off my old idea for a group of rogue pilots, updated it and made it into a more official squadron that Rita was flying for, and voila, Squadron 13 was open for business. Back in the day, I had outlined several possible stories set in and around the Caribbean, Central America and along the Mexican border. Adapting these for Rita's flying adventures was easy. "Frequency" was the first one. It worked out way better than I hoped.

So here we are back in volume 2 with another Rita adventure. In "Pick Up", Rita finds adventure south of the border. She's flying a new aircraft and has a new mission but she is still the bold, spunky flier we met and loved in Volume 1. The idea behind "Pick Up" is fairly straight-forward but you will still find plenty of flying scenes and what I hope is a lot of action on the ground and in the air.

This story was easy for me to write. It took some time but that was because of a lot of outside happenings not the actual writing which took only two weeks or so. Rita is a lot of fun, both to write and to read. I hope you like this new volume of her adventure. Will there be more volumes? Only Captain Ron knows for sure but a second volume is surely a good sign. I hope you enjoy reading “Pick Up” as much as I enjoyed writing it.

GENE MOYERS - Gene Moyers studied European and Medieval history at the University of Oregon. He is also a U.S. Army veteran. He worked in the high-tech industry for some time and is also a licensed massage therapist.

An avid military gamer and role player, his favorite game is *Daredevils* a pulp based roleplaying game set in the 1930s. His love affair with the 1930s and pulps in particular stem from his first time reading a *Shadow* novel as a boy. Although interested in writing since a teen he did not turn to serious writing until 2000.

He is the co-author of *GURPS Crusades* published by Steve Jackson Games. He has written several stories for Airship 27 including stories published in all of the *Purple Scar volumes,* all of the *Domino Lady volumes, Mystery Men and Women vol.5, The Phantom Detective vol.1, Moon Man vol. 2, The Legends of New Pulp Fiction and The adventures of Radio Rita vol. 1.* He has also written a story published in *Alternative Air Adventures* for Pro Se Publications and one published in *Gentlemen Prefer Domino Lady* for Moonstone Books.

When not working on various new pulp projects, he is busy writing alternate history stories or horror adventures for his occult investigator, the *Dream Master*. Gene currently lives in Beaverton, Oregon with his wife and two lazy dogs.

In Time

by Glen Held

Gunshots exploded in the air around them rocking the plane. A grim smile lit up Radio Rita's features. She always smiled in the face of death; especially when she had an ace up her sleeve.

Rita banked the AT-12 twin seat Guardsman sharply, turning the sturdy aircraft completely sideways to present a smaller target. Easing up on the accelerator, the plane began to plummet, heading for the mountain range below. As it went down, she saw two more wrecks scattered among the mountains. Added to the three she had previously seen, that meant five pilots had met their end here.

She didn't intend to be sixth.

"What are you doing, Rita?" the ghostly essence of what had been Mel Esposito called to her from the back seat. He had been complaining since the quartet of enemy fighters had risen out of the mountains ten minutes prior. "The Guardsman wasn't built for this kind of thing."

"It's okay," she said as their plane headed straight down. Above them, their attackers circled, trying to figure out what she was up to. Below them, the jagged peaks of the mountains were getting closer and closer.

"I don't like this, Rita!" Mel screamed.

"Trust me!" Rita said. She was so used to his presence, be it real or imagined, that she didn't question why a ghost would fear death.

Radio Rita's hands clutched the wheel as she kept the AT-12's nose pointed straight down. The enemy had stopped circling and began their descent. Her grin reappeared. This was exactly what she wanted.

"Nice knowing you!" Mel groaned.

"Hang on tight!" she yelled. "Here we go!"

Mel didn't even have time to scream as Rita cut the engines. The enemy stayed behind waiting for her to either pull up and out of the dive or smash to pieces on the mountaintop.

It was a smart move on their part.

It was also a wrong move.

With very little space between her and the mountain, Rita played her hand. Underneath the back of the plane she had installed an oval-shaped device that didn't look like anything much. What it was though was a third engine. Small and powerful, it would give the plane more maneuverability, although it could only be used once. Hopefully, once was all she needed. Flicking the extra engine switch on her control panel, the high-powered mechanism roared to life, causing the plane to immediately turn inwards, flying upside down bare feet over the top of the mountain.

Mel screamed and Rita howled in triumph as the plane curved completely around, blasting back up in the sky. The enemy, expecting her to turn in the other direction, were now above and ahead of her. Rita got two in her cross-hairs and shot them out of the sky. The other two, having lost their stomach for this fight, quickly banked away back into the mountains. She didn't go after them, instead getting back on her original flight plan. Radio Rita had a mission to complete.

"What just happened?" Mel asked, regaining his composure.

"They made the mistake of thinking their planes were as good as mine," Rita said sadly. "I wish they would have just let us cross their borders. We weren't harming anyone."

"Well, they learned their lesson the hard way," Mel said, his bravado returning after that near-death—for her at least—experience. "And chalk up two more kills for you."

Radio Rita blanched. The press and her fellow pilots had her pegged as a female shark of the skies and she hated it. All thirty-eight, now forty, of her kills had been justified.

"Despite what they say, I don't like killing and you know that, Mel," she explained. "I'll do it in self-defense, or when there's no other choice, but it makes me sick to my stomach."

Mel scoffed. "There are many people in heaven and hell who would disagree."

"How would you know?" Rita angrily snapped back. "It's not like you've been to either place, now is it?"

"That was unkind," Mel said sadly, then shimmered out of existence.

Rita sighed, regretting her words to the ghost, even if they were true. When, or if, Mel came back, she would apologize. Right now, she had a job to finish. Rita headed for the end of the mountain range and toward the small, picturesque eastern European kingdom of Belakoya. She looked at her watch. In twenty more minutes she would be there and find out what the *important* package she carried—and that caused the death of the two other pilots—was.

Radio Rita felt a slight chill in the air. A quick glance behind her showed what she already knew. The ghost of Mel had returned. She waited for him to say something as they flew out of the mountains and reached the outskirts of Belakoya, but he remained quiet.

"I'm glad you're back," she called to him. No response. "I'm sorry for what I said to you, Mel."

Still nothing. *Okay,* she thought, *if that's the way he's going to be, then she wouldn't talk to him either. She hadn't asked to be saddled with a ghost anyway.*

A few moments later they came to fields of crops and farmhouses. Mel whistled. "Well, don't that beat all," he said, breaking the silence.

"Wow!" Rita exclaimed. The scenery below was as brightly colored as that Wizard of Oz movie she'd gone to the premiere of a few nights earlier. Fields and buildings were so bright that it almost hurt her eyes to look at them. Every couple of miles though was a farm and farmhouse completely devoid of any color whatsoever. They looked like they belonged on the moon. "What do you make of all this?"

"No clue, but the city up ahead looks to be the same," Mel said, then let out a long whistle. "Will you look at the size of that castle up ahead! And those crazy colors! Probably killed a dozen rainbows painting that monstrosity!"

The building way off in the distance was big, probably two hundred feet tall, and painted in such vibrant colors that Rita got somewhat dizzy just looking at it. Now why would anyone build a castle like that? With war inevitably approaching, the place's size and vibrancy would make it a clear target for any...

Rita suddenly veered the plane away from the castle. "There's a garrison on the castle wall with their guns trained on us," she explained before Mel could question her. "They're not shooting, but I'm not taking any chances."

"Yikes!" Mel exclaimed. "Didn't that guy tell us at our meeting in New York to bring that package they gave you to King Kohler? How are we going to do that if they threaten to shoot us down?"

As Mel was invisible to everyone but her, there was no "us" or "our." There was only Rita. But after their recent argument, she didn't correct him. And what he said was otherwise correct. The man who came to her office at the almost completed LaGuardia airport had made a simple request: Bring a package to King Kohler at his castle in Belakoya.

Rita had been paid an obscene amount of money to transport her plane to Europe, then fly on a path they had outlined for her. Another large sum would be paid to her once she delivered the goods. No mention was made of planes trying to shoot her down, but given the tense climate in Eastern Europe, that really shouldn't have surprised her.

"Since I don't see any suitable place to land around here," Rita said, "I'll double back and set the Guardsman down on one of those fields."

About a mile away from the palace, she spotted a field she felt appropriate for landing. It was one of the monochrome lifeless ones where she wouldn't be destroying anyone's livelihood. She landed the Guardsman without so much as a bump. Rita and Mel got out of the flying machine—she going through her door, he wafting through his. From the cargo hold, she took out the shoebox-sized package she'd been paid to bring here.

"What do we do now?" Mel asked.

"Wait for someone to arrive and take us to the castle," she said. "With the amount of money King Kohler paid to have that package brought here, he's sure to send someone to meet us."

As they waited, Rita looked around. In the distance was a grey farmhouse. After a few seconds of staring, she was just able to make out a monochrome man and woman peering out a window at them. Rita went "psst" and motioned Mel to look that way. When he did, the pair disappeared into their depressing looking house, window shades slowly pulling shut behind them.

"Saint Peter gave me a friendlier reception after he looked me up in that book of his," Mel grumbled. Rita regarded him with a raised eyebrow. "Okay, I didn't actually get to the pearly gates, but you know what I mean."

Rita sighed once again not knowing if Mel was really a ghost or a figment of her imagination. Whatever he was, she was glad for his company in this weird place.

"Do you think we've waited long enough?" Mel asked five minutes later.

Radio Rita looked at her watch and sighed. "Yep. We haven't come all this way not to get paid."

After securing the plane, and with Rita carrying the package, the pair began to walk toward the castle. The farms they passed were all brightly painted with no rhyme or reason for their colors. The few times they encountered people tending the fields, the workers immediately scattered, hiding in the nearest barn or farmhouse.

Pretty soon they reached the city limit, the houses here all built the same and each garishly colored. The streets they lined were labyrinthian and eerily deserted. Although the castle loomed large in front of her, she had no idea how to get there through the twisting roads.

"Too bad you're not a normal flying ghost," Rita said to Mel.

"Nothing about me has ever been *normal*," Mel said. "Although, ghostwise, you know I have been able to possess people for a short period of time."

"So you say," Rita replied. "All I saw was people stop moving. To me they looked to be lost in thought."

"Possessed," Mel said firmly.

"Whatever," Rita replied, then heard something coming their way. It sounded like the neighing and hoofbeats of a horse. A moment later, a horse-drawn, multi-colored wagon came toward them. There were buckets of glistening paint and a trio of white-jump-suited painters in the vehicle: A big driver and a pale man, like the people she had seen at the monochrome farm, were up front while a solitary man sat in back.

"Excuse me," Rita called out and they stopped in front of her. "Do any of you speak English?"

"Everyone in Belakoya speaks English," the big driver proudly stated, his words slightly accented.

Rita smiled, hoping to get out of this weird place as quickly as possible. "Can you please tell me how to get to the castle?"

"Say something bad about Kohler," the pale painter growled causing the driver and man in the back to gasp. "Then you'll be taken there so fast your head will spin."

"Are you crazy, Ivan? Keep quiet!" The big driver's whisper was loud enough for her to hear. "Didn't you learn your lesson?"

"No, I've been quiet long enough," Ivan snarled.

"You've been anything but quiet and look where it's gotten you!" The big driver indicated Ivan's pallid body. "One more time will mean your end!"

"I don't know what's going on here," Mel whispered to Rita, "but I don't like it. I'm going to try and possess them and find out." The ghost vanished.

Rita sighed, then addressed Ivan. "Isn't Kohler a good king? From everything we've seen in America, Kohler is loved by all..."

The pale man's laugh interrupted her. "Loved?"

"Stay silent," the biggest hissed.

"He's a tyrant! There's nothing good about him!" Ivan's face grew only slightly red even though he was obviously furious. He waved around him. "See all this? It's not real! Phony! Kohler only lets the outside world see what he wants them to see!"

Radio Rita did not like what she was hearing. All the newsreels she'd seen of the kingdom showed happy villagers amidst storybook-like homes. Although she hadn't encountered any of that happiness, she hadn't seen otherwise either...until now.

"Then why isn't anyone else complaining?" Rita asked.

"Because of what he can do to us! He..."

"Take him in the back, Donal!" the big driver snarled and nodded to the third man who had said nothing before. "Hey! Did you hear me? What's wrong with you?"

The third painter, Donal, shook himself as if coming out of a stupor. Once he was composed, he quickly pulled a non-struggling Ivan in back with him.

"You want to visit our majestic highness, yes?" the big man said quickly. "You can find he who is the sun and the stars by making the first left up ahead, then go down two blocks and turn right. That will lead you into the marketplace.

The castle entrance is through there."

"All hail King Kohler!" Donal chimed in. Ivan said it as well but without gusto. Then the driver cracked his reigns and the horse drove them away.

"This Kohler sounds like a real winner," Mel said, having returned to Rita's side. She nodded. "By the way, you saw I took over the body of the one in the back, didn't you?"

"I saw he wasn't moving," Rita said, not wanting to again engage in this with him. "As far as the king goes, we'd better be careful. This place obviously isn't what we thought."

"Agreed," Mel said as they followed the big driver's directions. "It seems they disguise their unhappiness with bright colors."

"Could be, but I think there's something else going on here; something disturbing. I think it best if we deliver our goods and get out of here as quick as possible."

"Yes, ma'am," Mel said, and they made their way into the marketplace, which was filled not only with color, but people engaged in buying and selling. They were animatedly speaking a language she couldn't understand but fell silent when the pair entered.

"Oh come on," Rita said, admonishing them. "Seriously?"

"Maybe they've never seen a tall redheaded pilot hanging around with such a handsome ghost," Mel said. Rita couldn't help but chuckle at that.

There was a commotion and the crowd parted to reveal a half dozen brightly decorated soldiers on horses. A storybook coach was pulled by the last of them and stopped before her. One of the soldiers dismounted and opened the carriage door.

"Enter," he commanded. "King Kohler wishes your presence."

"Well, this is more like it!" Mel said and went into the carriage. Rita entered behind him, the guard closed the door, and they were off. She looked behind her as they went through the marketplace and toward the festive-looking castle. Although the people remained silent, everywhere she looked their faces showed fear.

Rita's mouth fell open as she and Mel entered the cavernous throne room. They were ushered in front of a huge throne dripping with enough diamonds and other precious jewels to keep everyone in the country prosperous for the rest of their lives. The room itself was decked out with golden statues, masterpiece artwork and fine tapestries enough to provide extreme wealth for the lifetimes of their children and grandchildren as well.

"We should have asked for more money to bring that box here," Mel whispered, indicating the package that Rita still held onto.

"Will you be quiet," Rita warned him in a low tone.

"Aw, they can't hear…"

"Silence!" one of the king's colorful soldiers, and there were ten on each side of the aisle leading up to the throne, roared.

Mel fell silent and Rita's eyes grew wide. Had the guard said that to her or had he heard the ghost speak? Her questions were drowned out by a fanfare of trumpets and then a pair of mismatched looking men entered. One was short and squat, arms dangling well past his knees, head and body covered in wild grey hair. The other was tall and slender, a touch of grey in his temples, and carrying an oversized, gaily painted book. The shorter man stood to the right of the throne, the other to the left. Once they were in place, an unseen band began to play "Begin the Beguine."

"Is this for real?" Mel whispered. Before Rita could respond, there was a puff of smoke out of which a heavyset man in his late thirties emerged. From the long mink robe he wore to his shining crown to the air of superiority around him, there was no doubt this was King Kohler.

Moving in time with the song, Kohler went around the throne then sat. The taller of the two men flanking him began to speak, but the king put up a hand stopping him. Kohler closed his eyes and swayed to the music. Only after it was done did he open his eyes and nod for the man to proceed.

"All stand in awe before His royal highness," the taller man bellowed, his voice echoing throughout the chamber, "master of all he surveys, he of the genius intellect and beloved of his people, King Kohler of Belakoya!"

The guards beat on their chests with their right hands and the two advisors clapped with enthusiasm. "When in Rome," Rita said and clapped as well.

King Kohler smiled taking it all in, then gave a signal immediately stopping the accolades. He looked at Rita, his eyes going up and down her. She tried very hard not to show how much the action repulsed her.

"I'm so glad you were the one to get past those horrible mountain fliers from the next country." He gave a theatrical shiver. "I would hate to think of Radio Rita scattered in pieces throughout the mountainside."

She looked quizzically at the king. "What are you talking about? Are you telling me you had other pilots doing this task as well?"

King Kohler chuckled, the rest of the court immediately joining him. "You didn't think you were the only one I entrusted to bring a package to me, did you?" he asked. "There were four others, but you were the first and only one to get through which actually saves us a lot of trouble in deciding who goes on from here."

"This place gives me the creeps," Mel said. "Let's get our money and get out of here."

Rita nodded slightly. "No offense to you and your kingdom, your highness," she said, keeping her voice well-modulated, "but, if you don't mind, I'd like to be paid and then I'll get on my way. I've been away from home a long time."

"Of course, of course." The king gave a dismissive wave of his hand. "First let's make sure that everything is in order with my package. Can't be too careful these days."

"Is he saying we pulled a fast one?" Mel pounded a ghostly fist into a ghostly hand. "I should try and possess him."

"The king has every right to inspect his property," Rita said, addressing both the ghost and the king.

Kohler nodded royally. "I do, don't I? But first..." He nodded to the foremost guard who, in turn, pointed to two other guards who then hurried from the room. "Before we open my package, let's hear a little something about you."

"What is it you want to know?" Rita asked.

King Kohler gave her an odd look. "I don't want to hear from you, my dear," he stated. "Whatever you would say is biased. Mr. Creeks will provide all the information I need in a non-partisan manner. Mr. Creeks!"

"I'm liking this king guy less and less," Mel whispered.

"That makes two of us," Radio Rita shot back.

Mr. Creeks, the tall man holding the large, diamond covered tome, stepped forward. He cleared his throat, then thumbed through the book until he got to the page he wanted. "Rita Calahan, also known as 'Radio' Rita is twenty-seven, born on Long Island of lower middle-class parents. Her father was an electrician, her mother a teacher. Rita graduated high school with perfect grades and excelled in track and field. She was offered a scholarship to Bryn Mawr College in Pennsylvania, but she fell in love with planes, and a pilot, while watching a summer barnstormer show. Rita subsequently ran away from home to join the show, throwing away her scholarship and breaking her parents' hearts."

"Ouch!" Mel cringed at the words.

"Ah, the folly of youth." Kohler made a tsk-tsk noise, then brightened. "But I too was quite reckless in my early days, although I did attend one of the top colleges in your country, where I was a revered scholar. Now here I sit, the smartest man in the country and lord of all I survey!"

The guards and the dignitaries all began to clap. This time Rita didn't join in. Instead, she stood there, silently fuming over the bad memories Mr. Creeks and his book were dredging up. At another nod from Kohler, the dignitary continued.

"Although the lead pilot subsequently left her, Rita stayed with the show and learned everything there was to know about planes from a pilot viewpoint as well as an engineering one. In her early twenties, she left the show to start her own company. She now chauffeurs celebrities and dignitaries as well as taking on jobs too tough for other pilots to handle.

"Of particular note is one such piloting job where she was entrusted with flying a low-level mobster across country after he gave testimony to a senate committee on racketeering."

"Hey, they're talking about me!" Mel said, brightening up.

"Unfortunately, that ended in disaster. Where she was taking him was leaked and the pair were met with a dozen revenge minded mobsters. Although Rita gamely tried to fight them off, her passenger was ultimately killed."

"Boy, you should have seen her!" Mel exclaimed, throwing imaginary blows. "She fought like a wildcat! I never saw anything like it."

"Some say that Rita now has the spirit of Mel Esposito, the dead man, travelling with her," Mr. Creeks continued. "Whether he really is a spirit, or a manifestation of her guilt, is unknown." The man closed the book and stepped back.

King Kohler sat forward in his chair. "Is he here now?" he asked, looking around them. "The ghost I mean."

"How do you know all this?" Rita asked, her face red over everything that had been divulged.

"He's here now, isn't he!" Kohler clapped his hands. "How I wish I had finished my spectral viewing glasses, but when you have so many ideas as I do, some just—"

Kohler stopped as the two guards returned. One of them carried a sturdy square table. The other held a small rectangular box with a paper seal around it. The table was set up in front of the king, the rectangular box put on a corner of that.

"We'll have time for the ghost later," the king declared. "Right now, I'd like to inspect the package to find if you did indeed pass your test. Put the box you were entrusted with on the table, please, and let's hope it fared better in your care than poor Mel Esposito."

"What test?" Mel asked, but Rita said nothing. There was more going on here than just a delivery. Rita put the package she had brought from America on the table.

Kohler motioned Rita back, then walked over to the box and inspected the lock. Satisfied it had not been tampered with, he called over Mr. Abbot who put in the right combination. There was a click and the top of the box flung open, a cloud of cold smoke wafting out of it. Mr. Abbot moved away, and Kohler lifted his arms at the elbows. A pair of guards raced over and put long rubber gloves on him, while another placed thick goggles over the king's eyes.

"Is he here now? The ghost I mean."

Once properly outfitted, his royal highness came forward again to stand before the box. Looking at Rita, then downward, he suddenly plunged his hands into the smoking innards, screaming out in pain as he did. Rita and Mel looked at each other in alarm, but the king broke their panic when a smile lit up his face.

"Got you!" Kohler said.

"Not funny," Rita declared. The guards glared at her, but the king shrugged, and took a container from the package.

The guards closed the outer box and took it away while Kohler had his gloves and glasses removed. "Come here, Rita, and bring the ghost with you," he said, barely holding in a chuckle. Rita silently went to his side. Mel came with her.

"Ah, I am literally drooling at the mouth over this," Kohler opened the box with the seal and held up its contents.

"A spoon?"

"Nothing gets past you, does it?" Kohler then opened the container so Rita couldn't see it. A fruity smell filled the air and the king's stomach gurgled. Then he dipped the spoon into the mixture and held up a semi-frozen confection. He put it in his mouth.

"Ah," he moaned, "strawberry ice cream!"

"Uh, oh," Mel saw Rita's face fill with anger.

"You mean that four pilots lost their lives because you wanted strawberry ice cream?" Radio Rita snapped.

"Those pilots had the same chance to survive as you did." The king took another bite, rolling his eyes as he ate.

"Four men are lying dead on top of that mountain for a container of ice cream?" she asked, barely containing her growing anger.

"But it's very, very good!" The king licked his lips. "Totally worth it!"

"Then so is this," Rita said, and what she did next changed the course of many lives.

"Did you really have to do that, Rita?" Mel's voice called from the semi-darkness.

"Don't start with me, Mel Esposito," Rita snarled. "He deserved much worse than what I gave him."

She heard Mel sigh. "I'm not saying you're wrong, but—"

"Good," she cut him off. It didn't stop him.

"*But*," he continued, "you had to figure that punching a king in the face would have consequences."

She snorted. "At the time, I didn't really care."

"How about now?"

Rita didn't respond. Instead, she walked the perimeter of their prison, trying to find a way out. The cell was about twenty feet by twenty feet, surrounded by walls on three sides, the other by metal bars spaced close enough that she couldn't get her shapely body through them. The floor was covered with straw, the only light coming in from a barred window about seven feet off the ground.

There was no way out.

Rita sighed and sat on the floor under the window. Mel seated himself next to her. "I honestly don't know what to do next."

Mel nodded. "Let's go over what we do know. Maybe that will help."

So Rita reviewed what had happened. Immediately after striking the king, a quartet of guards whisked Kohler away, the rest descended on Rita. She fought back, fists and feet flying, but it was a losing battle. Mel was too excited to possess anyone and tried to fight, but his spectral form had no effect on flesh and blood. Within minutes, the guards had captured Rita. They seemed about to kill her until Mr. Abbot ordered them to take her to the dungeon; King Kohler wanted personal revenge. Scared of the king's wrath, the guards followed Mr. Abbot's orders, Mel going along with her. That had been half a day ago.

"I don't think that helped," she wearily said.

Mel tried to put his arm around Rita, but it passed through her. He sighed, then got up and went to the prison's bars. "If only—" A pulsating red glow coming from the cell across the way stopped him. "What the devil is that?"

Rita came to his side and peered into the glow. "I can't make it out." Then she heard a whirring noise coming from the eerie illumination.

"Something's happening to me!" Mel suddenly cried. "Something bad!"

Turning back to him, Rita saw that Mel had begun to change! Like a piece of saltwater taffy, he was being stretched, one side of his ghostly form being pulled through the bars and toward the whirring.

"Hellllp meeee…" Mel cried as more of him headed away. He held out his arm to her and Rita grabbed for her friend, but his insubstantiality made those actions futile.

"Stop it!" she screamed toward whatever was doing this. Her words, like her actions, had no impact.

"Pleeease," he said, a tear coming from his stretched-out visage. "It huuurtssss…"

And then the whirring sound was gone *and so was Mel.*

"Mel! Mel!" she cried.

"Pull yourself together," a voice said from the darkness in front of her cell, "we've got important work to do." Then a match was struck, a candle lit, and Mr.

Abbot appeared out of nowhere.

"Where did you come from?" she asked, regaining her composure. "And what happened to Mel?"

"There's not much time, so listen closely if you want to continue living," he said, disregarding her question. "If you agree to do a job for me, I will get you out of here and return your ghost to you."

"What have you done to him?" Rita's arms shot through the bars grabbing at him. But Mr. Abbot was perfectly placed, her reach falling just short of him.

Mr. Abbot turned his candle toward the other cell. Inside it, partially covered by spider webs, was a three foot tall, metal creature. It had a ball for a head, tank-like treads for feet, thin rods for arms and an oblong torso. There was no face, just a faded number seven painted on it. The eerie crimson glow came from inside a transparent window on the thing's torso. Something was swirling around inside it. Rita's heart skipped a beat as the swirling mass stopped moving and she realized what it was...

It was Mel.

"What did you do to him?"

"I did nothing, but I see by your actions that number seven must have done something," Mr. Abbot said. "That machine, originally built by King Kohler and the last of its kind, was reprogrammed by me to imprison, and eventually break down, any ghostly essence within twenty feet. I'll let him out, but only after you help me."

Rita glared at the short man. "Help you do what?"

"I want you to fly me somewhere and drop me off," Mr. Abbot continued. "Once you do that, you can go on your way, and I'll remotely shut off number seven which will free your ghost."

Rita thought quickly. "Your country must have pilots, so the fact you're unwilling to use them, means you don't want me, you *need* me."

"I do. I don't trust any of our pilots and, even if I did, none of them have your skills."

Rita's eyes bore into Mr. Abbot. "Then let my friend go now and you have my word I'll help you so long as your task doesn't hurt innocent people."

"You make a good point, but there's something you don't know that gives me the upper hand. Look outside and best to hurry. It's not like killing ghosts is an exact science. Yours could be dissolved at any moment."

Rita went to the window, then jumped to grab hold of the bars. Hoisting herself up, the pilot looked out to see a large courtyard where a six-foot-tall wooden X had been erected. Next to that, a structure that looked like gallows was being set up. There were about twenty rows of chairs behind them.

"That's what Kohler has planned for you, and ticket sales to watch your execution are going fast!" Mr. Abbot told her. "So, unless you want to swing by your pretty little neck, I suggest you take my offer which gives you at least some chance at survival."

He was right. "Okay, we have a deal."

Mr. Abbot smiled. "I'll be back." Then he and the light vanished as suddenly as they had arrived.

Ten minutes after Mr. Abbot's disappearing act, the door to the prison opened and light flowed in. Rita got to her feet just as a half dozen of King Kohler's armed guards marched into the prison. A mustachioed man, their leader, threw a pair of handcuffs through her bars.

"Put them on, the king wants to see you," the guard said. When Rita hesitated, he aimed his gun at her. "Die here or out there. It doesn't matter to me."

Reluctantly, Rita put the cuffs on. While she did, she saw a young guard investigate the cell across from her. "Hey, there's one of those old automatons! Number seven! The last one made," he said joyfully as he pointed at the mechanical man. As none of them said anything about a ghost, Rita knew they couldn't see Mel. "Don't the history books say that King Kohler had all of them destroyed after he returned from college?"

"They do, so we'll notify the king of it being down here. In the meantime, stay away from it. Those things were supposed to be deadly," the lead guard warned, but the other wasn't taking his advice and entered the opposite cell.

"I always wanted to see one of these. I wonder if it still works." The young guard bent down to check it out. As he did the whirring sound returned. "It does!"

That was the last thing he said as a trio of blades came out of the end of the rods and began spinning like propellers. "Get out!" the mustachioed guard cried, but it was too late. With a savage thrust, the blades cut into the young guard's throat, sending him to the ground with a gurgling noise. He twitched twice, then lay still. The blades went back into the rods and the whirring stopped. Another guard quickly slammed that cell door shut.

Walking glumly, the guards escorted Rita out of the prison, keeping far away from the opposing cell as they left. Up a staircase they went into the courtyard past the almost completed gallows. A few moments later, they were back in the castle and headed for the throne room. They stopped as Mr. Creeks came running toward them.

"Change of plans," Creeks said. "King Kohler wants her in the picture room."

"But I was told—" The mustachioed guard stopped when he saw the stern look on Creeks' face. "We will take the prisoner to the picture room."

"Hail Kohler!" Creeks said and left as the guards returned the sentiment.

The procession backtracked a bit then led Rita up a flight of steps to a big room with a vaulted ceiling. From top to bottom, the walls were covered with pictures of King Kohler performing heroic actions, none of which Rita believed to be true. There was a throat clearing and Rita directed her attention to the front of the room where Kohler himself sat upon a throne. There was a bandage across his nose and his eyes were puffy from where Rita had hit him.

"Your time in the dungeon is just the start of what I'm going to do to you!" he hissed. She made a fake move toward him, and he flinched. That gave her a lot of satisfaction, even with the resultant painful jabbing of something in her back by the guards.

"Chain her to the chair!" a red-faced Kohler ordered his men. "Do it quickly, or you'll be swinging in the courtyard with her!"

There was a plain chair in front of the king which the guards hurriedly pushed her onto and did as ordered. Soon, she was bound hand and foot, completely unable to move. Rita stoically endured this, all the while looking for an escape route... or a way to sell her life dearly.

"You're sure she's fastened securely?" the king asked, and the mustachioed guard pulled her chains tight. The bonds cut into her, and she grimaced. "Good, now go."

"Leave?" the leader of the guards asked. "But, sire, even tied up she's dangerous."

"Don't provoke me!" the king snapped, and the guards all bowed to him. He put out his hand. "Give me the key to her chains and go. I will talk with her in private."

The king's stern look stopped any further questioning. The keys were handed over and Kohler pointed to the door. The men looked to their mustachioed leader who shrugged and nodded toward the portal. They all marched to it, the mustachioed leader looking back once more to make sure his liege hadn't changed his mind. Kohler made a shooing motion, and the man did, closing the door behind him.

The king hurried past her, and Rita could hear him locking the door from the inside. Then he came to face her. "Let's get to work."

Rita laughed sarcastically. "If you think I'm going to help you, you're—" She stopped talking as the man's body began to shimmer, his features changing to that of Mr. Abbot.

"Hurry," he said, unlocking her chains, "we've got no time to lose!"

"Mr. Abbot?" Rita questioned, not believing her eyes.

"Yes, it's me," he answered. "I—" The older man stopped as they heard talking outside the door. "We've got to go! The guards could come back at any moment, and I don't have enough energy to use the disguise machine again after being Creek and Kohler."

Without another word, the man took her hand and led her to a painting of a massively muscled King Kohler standing victoriously over two heavily wounded foes. There were another three on the ground that he appeared to have dispatched. The old man walked right for the painting, his pace not slowing. Radio Rita tried to get away, but the man held tight, dragging her forward.

"What are you doing?" Rita asked.

"Have faith and shut your eyes," he ordered, and she did. Rita expected to bounce off the wall, but that didn't happen. Instead, she grew nauseous, her mind tilting ninety degrees, then back again. When she opened her eyes she was…somewhere else.

"What just happened?" Rita queried, looking around. They were in an old-fashioned laboratory, with bubbling concoctions, machinery shooting off electrical charges, and rows of chemicals and minerals stretching up and down the walls. There was even a large fish tank-like cage filled with hamsters running on treadmills. The strangest part were the colors in the laboratory which were even richer than those of the castle.

Mr. Abbot released his hold on her. "We are in my hidden lab, one step out of time with reality."

"Oh, that explains everything," Rita said sarcastically. "Come on, be straight with me."

"Yes, it's time for explanations," he sighed. "I am chief scientist of Belakoya as was my father and his father before that. The difference being that my ancestors worked for honorable royalty, whereas I work for a callous, narcissist of a dictator who not only does nothing to help his people but threatens them with unknown tortures if they don't constantly praise him to the heavens."

"Okay, you don't like Kohler and I can't blame you for that," Rita said, "but what does that have to do with our current predicament?"

Mr. Abbot nodded. "Let me just attend to a few matters then I'll explain more thoroughly."

"Wait for *what* to be ready?" she asked, but Mr. Abbot didn't answer. Instead, he became deeply involved with the multitude of contraptions lining his lab.

Trying to stay out of his way, Radio Rita went to the only window in the place and was shocked by what she saw. Outside was a view of her plane *in the field where she had landed*. Compared to the brightness of the room, the picture looked as if it were in black and white, but that wasn't what astonished her the most. That would be that the Guardsman looked like it was no more than fifty yards away, although her still aching feet assured her it was miles away.

"How am I able to see my plane from here? And how does it look so close?"

"Keep watching," Mr. Abbot, not looking up from his machinations, replied.

Rita returned her gaze to the window and saw that the view had changed. In front of her now was the marketplace, full of people and activity. As she continued to watch, it changed again so that she was seeing inside the prison cells where a pained Mel was inside the automaton. Then the view turned to other parts of the kingdom.

"This isn't a window," she finally reasoned. "It's some sort of picture receiver."

"Correct," Mr. Abbot concurred. "Now let me finish as King Kohler will no doubt soon decipher what has happened and take steps to stop us."

Rita scoffed. "You think your idiot king will figure out something this complicated? He didn't seem like he had enough brainpower to blow out a candle."

Mr. Abbot sighed again. "Which is exactly what he wants you to think so you will underestimate him. Kohler is a beyond brilliant scientist. He designed the automatons as well as the receiver/window and the mechanism that got us into our current predicament."

"What predicament?"

"You've obviously seen all the colors around here, as well as the lack of color," Mr. Abbot pointed out. Rita nodded. "Years ago, Kohler foolishly experimented with forces he didn't understand opening a breach into a monochromatic universe devoid of emotions. Whatever lives there acquired a taste for our life forces—human, plant, and animal—and started to drain us, turning our kingdom into a dreary black and white wasteland.

"Seeing he couldn't contain them, Kohler came to me for help. Our combined intellects came up with a way to stop this incursion. I won't bore you with the technicalities, but we were able to temporarily close the dimensional doorway about ninety-eight percent. To keep them from invading again, we did two things. First, we developed a vibrantly colored paint that wards off their attacks by being too rich for them to ingest. King Kohler withholds the paint to keep his subjects in line.

"Second, through trial and error, we have worked out an acceptable loss number wherein we don't use the paint all the time and let the other dimensional beings take some of what they crave. This has staved off a full-fledged attack, but what they want seems to grow every year as does their ferocity.

"Although there's little doubt the creatures will one day launch another full-fledged attack, the king has blocked anyone from going for help: He does not want the outside world to vilify him as surely they will once this leeching extends beyond our borders. To that end, he allows me to experiment with ideas to stop this purge, giving me freedom to secretly invent things like this room and expand on his inventions such as the invisibility shield."

Rita regarded Mr. Abbot with an arched eyebrow. "This is all a little far-fetched."

Mr. Abbot scoffed. "Says the woman who thinks she hangs around with a ghost."

Rita winced. "True, but—"

"I thought you'd have doubts, so I've prepared proof. Come."

Mr. Abbot motioned Rita over to the hamster cage where the animals were happily going about their business. He wheeled over a water tank and hooked it up to a hose leading to the top of the cage. Putting on thick multi-colored gloves, he then used a cup to scoop out some of the liquid. He held the glass out to her.

Rita's expression turned to disgust. "No thanks."

"Okay, I just wanted to show you that this is ordinary water." He bent at the waist and carefully took a swig, being careful not to spill it. "See? Just plain water."

"Duly noted," Rita didn't know why he was making such a fuss.

The man smiled. "Good, now watch."

Mr. Abbot turned a mechanism on top of the tank, causing a motor to hum, then moved back. Not knowing what was about to happen, but choosing to exercise caution, Radio Rita moved away as well. A moment later, a fine mist sprayed down onto the hamsters. Where it touched them, the color drained away from the small creatures and their movements became lethargic. When the water finished coming down, the hamsters were now both totally devoid of color and barely moving. Soon, they were not moving at all.

"What did you do to them?" Rita asked.

"With their protective coloring gone, the other dimension was able to leach their life force. You're okay to go near it since you haven't been here long enough to be affected," he stated. "I'm probably safe being in this room, but I'd rather not get close until the cage thoroughly drains."

Rita couldn't believe what she was seeing. "How do you bathe? What do you do when it rains? How were you able to drink the water?"

"As long as we are in our multi-colored houses, we are protected from the other dimensional forces and can bathe and drink freely. When it rains, Kohler projects an invisible shield of his own invention above Belakoya that keeps us safe. Even so, we only go into the rain when necessary and in paint treated rain gear. Since the paint is manufactured by Kohler and administered by his hand-picked crews, the people have little choice but to stay here and treat Kohler with respect he does not deserve."

He wheeled over a water tank and hooked it up to a hose...

“That’s horrible,” Rita said, “but how can my piloting skill possibly help against beings from another dimension?”

“In and of itself, you can’t, but you are a means to an end,” Mr. Abbot explained. “Since we have no way to fight the monsters, and odds are they will breach our barriers sooner than later, the only real solution is to make it so that they never came here in the first place.”

Rita scoffed. “You don’t need a plane for that, you need a time machine.”

“Which we have. Unfortunately, the portal it opens is not much bigger than your plane, stays open for only a few seconds and is five thousand feet in the sky. The king arranged for pilots to come here, not to deliver ice cream, but to go through that needle hole of a portal with one of his men. Once in the past, Kohler’s agent would meet his younger self and give information about the future including what he erroneously thinks to be a safe way to open the portal.”

Rita shivered. “I shudder to think what a man like Kohler would do with knowledge of the future.”

Mr. Abbot nodded. “Exactly, which is why I commandeered the time machine and have pinpointed the place in time in which I can stop Kohler’s plans.”

“When and where is that?”

“It is five years before the young king opened the door to the other dimension. Kohler was in college in New Jersey, and, although his authorized biography doesn’t say it, I’ve learned that something occurred there that kept him from realizing the danger of opening that doorway.”

“That’s not much to go on.”

Mr. Abbot agred. “I know, but I’ll figure out more when you drop me off there.”

Rita took a breath, then let it out slowly. “I don’t like the thought of messing with time, but I like King Kohler in power here even less so…” she paused, then smiled grimly.

“Let’s do it!”

Sticking to hidden passages and untraveled corridors, Rita and Mr. Abbot were able to make it through the castle without incident. Mr. Abbot had set the time machine to go on in exactly one hour. That left a little under fifty minutes to make it to the Guardsman, get it out of hiding and fly through the tiny time portal.

That wasn’t going to be easy. Wanted posters with Rita’s face and a reward for information leading to her capture were now plastered all over the castle and probably the entire kingdom. The reward wasn’t in money, but in cans of paint.

Rita knew that, even if the people didn't like Kohler, that paint meant life and they'd turn on her in a heartbeat.

The place where they were to exit the castle led into the courtyard. Rita felt Mr. Abbot move uncomfortably close and her stomach suddenly began to churn.

"I turned on the invisibility device so you might feel a bit queasy," he said, explaining his actions and her nausea.

The scene in front of Rita explained why he had done so. The empty chairs she had previously seen in the courtyard were now filled with multi-colored people. Twenty rows with ten on each side of a middle aisle meant two hundred witnesses sitting in front of the gallows and the X; two hundred people between them and the way out to the left side of the gallows sat King Kohler, his guards and Mr. Creek. Kohler and the guards wore dark wraparound sunglasses, and were constantly scanning the crowd and surrounding areas. As for the people, they were grumbling to each other, a sense of impending doom filling the air.

"Why are they all here?" Rita asked. "It doesn't make sense since they know I'm not their captive anymore and there won't be a hanging."

"This isn't for you, it's for him!" Mr. Abbot replied. "Look!"

Rita followed where the old man pointed. Guards were bringing in a struggling man. They headed for the big wooden X and strapped him onto it by his wrists and ankles. Rita recognized him immediately. It was Ivan, the painter who had made the bad comment about the king. His pale features were even more bleached out and he looked scared to death. Mr. Creek stood and produced a scroll from which he read Ivan's "sins" against the kingdom. When Creek finished, a man dressed like a fireman, with a long, rubberized coat, high boots, and a short in the front/long in the back hat walked down the middle aisle. He was dragging a hose with him. The crowd cheered at his entrance.

"What's going on?" Rita asked.

"I think it's our way out," Mr. Abbot said. "We can use the execution as a distraction to get out of here."

"Execution?" Rita realized that Ivan, much like the hamsters, was going to be doused with water allowing the other dimension to claim his life force.

"Does the condemned man have anything to say?" the fireman, stopping ten feet from the prisoner, questioned.

Ivan stopped struggling and passionately addressed the crowd. "Help me! I'm innocent I tell you! If you don't help me, then you'll be next! Mark my words, you'll be next!" he yelled, but nobody in the audience was moved by his words.

"Does anyone have anything to say in favor of the blasphemer?" the fireman called out. Under Kohler's gaze, and with the guards having pulled out their weapons, there was complete silence. "Then let the righting of the kingly wrong began!"

"When the dousing starts, we should be able—" Mr. Abbot began.

"No," Rita interrupted, thinking of the hamster's grizzly demise. "I can't let him suffer."

"You must!" argued Mr. Abbot. "Our task is too important to worry about one man."

Rita grabbed Mr. Abbot's arm in an unrelenting grip and walked toward the gathered crowd. "You can't do this!" Mr. Abbot hissed.

Rita bristled at the words, even as she moved ahead. "Watch me."

Pulling Mr. Abbot along with her, Rita picked up the pace, still not sure of what she was going to do. All she knew was that she wouldn't allow Ivan to be hurt, especially as it was somewhat her fault he was in this situation. If she hadn't questioned him about King Kohler, the hapless painter wouldn't be awaiting certain death.

Although none of the crowd noticed them as they walked down the middle aisle, the situation gave Rita a bad feeling. She looked up at King Kohler who seemed to be grinning at her. That could not be good. She stopped walking and took a few steps backward. Stopping abruptly, she took another few steps forward. A chill swept over her. The king's gaze had followed her whenever she changed directions.

"They see us," Rita whispered to Mr. Abbot.

"It's the glasses!" he whispered back. "Kohler must have known I took the invisibility device, so he equipped himself and the guards with the spectacles that allow them to see us! Look the guards are coming our way! What are we going to do?"

That was a very good question. Before she could think of an answer, Kohler's voice called out to her. "I knew you'd try to save poor Ivan!" he cried. People looked around wondering who their liege was talking to and hoping it wasn't them. "Your altruistic abilities are commendable, but foolish in the extreme."

"We're doomed," Mr. Abbot moaned.

"No, we're not. Quickly, tell me what happens if people get a little water on them? Will it kill them?"

"No. It will sting, but unless they're like Ivan, it will take a lot to—"

"That's all I need to know."

Rita grabbed Mr. Abbot by the arm and dragged him toward the fireman. Meanwhile, the guards kept coming toward them, knocking people over as they did. The crowd began to panic even though King Kohler screamed for them to remain calm, or they would all be punished.

Rita released Mr. Abbot when they got to the fireman. "Run!" she ordered.

"Meet me at the plane."

"If I move from you, everyone will see—"

Rita pushed him away, breaking their connection and their conversation. Since she couldn't see him any longer, she didn't know if he did what she asked, but she had other matters to attend. People pointed at her and screamed since, to their eyes, she appeared out of nowhere. As she came into view, the guards all raced forward. That was exactly what she was hoping for.

Rita took hold of the fire-hose pulling the instrument out of the stunned fireman's hands. Before anyone could react, she aimed the hose upward, and then pulled back its handle. An explosion of water burst out of it and into the sky. As it did, the people started to scream and race from their seats.

"Stay calm!" Kohler roared, but the immediate fear of the water hitting them overcame their fear of him.

Rita sprayed the approaching guards, who screamed in pain and raced away. One dropped his sword and, still holding the hose. She picked it up and went over to Ivan. Raising the weapon over her head then swinging it downward, she cut away his bonds, freeing the man from the X.

"My plane is out in the farthest black and white field," she said, still spraying water all around. "What's the quickest way there?"

"That way." Ivan pointed through the courtyard to an exit. "I'll take you."

"Good. On my signal." She lifted the sword on high again and cut the end of the hose off. Rita dropped it on the floor, the tube shooting water and writhing on the ground as if it were a snake in agony. "Go!"

"Turn off the water!" King Kohler roared from a safe distance.

As the guards jumped to obey, Rita and Ivan joined the crowd which was racing out of the palace grounds. Initially, she had to help Ivan, but he seemed to grow stronger upon entering the marketplace. They followed the crowd which tore through the venders, trampling their wares.

"I don't think anyone will turn us in," Ivan said, noticing that some in the crowd were looking at them, "but, then again, I didn't think my own crew would and, well, you saw what happened to me."

"Kohler seems to inspire fear-driven loyalty." Rita's voice was harsh. Even if the opportunity to try and get the king out of power hadn't presented itself, she would have had to have done something. She couldn't have left the kingdom without trying to help the people there.

"A few of us fight against him, but you see what happens when we do." Ivan led her out of the marketplace and into the farmlands. "He would have obliterated me if you hadn't acted when you did. For that I can only say thank you. I am in your debt."

"You're welcome," she said as he took them through the farmlands. Soon, she saw the monochromatic farm and her plane. The cover was still on, so she knew the Guardsman was untampered with. Rita looked at her watch. There were a little over ten minutes left in the hour. Good! She should be able to uncover the craft and take off as soon as Mr. Abbot arrived.

As Rita got to the plane, she heard a disembodied voice. "Thank heavens you're here. There's no time to lose!" Mr. Abbot appeared out of nowhere. He looked at Ivan, his eyes going wide. "You brought…"

Mr. Abbot didn't say anything further as Ivan let out a yelp of surprise… then punched the inventor square on the jaw. The older man let out a surprised 'oomph', then fell to the ground unmoving. Rita bent down and tried to wake him up, but Mr. Abbot was out for the foreseeable future.

"What did you do that for?" Rita growled, looking up angrily at Ivan.

"That's Abbot! He works for the king!" Ivan exclaimed.

"I can't believe you did that!" She stood up to go face to face with Ivan. "He and I were working together to save the kingdom!"

Ivan's jaw fell open. "Really?" he asked, and she nodded. "Well, how was I supposed to know? He appeared out of nowhere."

Rita kicked at the ground. "Great, just great!" She angrily began to take the tarp off the plane. "Now I'm going to have to do this all by myself and I don't have any idea what I'm doing!"

"Maybe I can help." Ivan said, following her around the plane. "Tell me everything Abbot told you."

"Why not?" Rita shrugged. "Believe it or not, we were supposed to go through a time portal to when Kohler was in college in New Jersey and, once there, do *something* to prevent him from realizing what would happen if he opened that dimensional doorway. I have zero idea what that would be."

Ivan smiled at her. "Believe it or not, I think I might know."

Rita finished taking off the tarp and packing it away. "How?"

"All of us here are forced to learn every facet of King Kohler's life. I know exactly where he went to school as well as other things concerning his life. Take me with you and we can figure this out together."

Once again, Rita found herself without a choice. "Let's go," she said, and they both got onto the plane.

Radio Rita checked her watch. It was about three minutes before the rip in time was supposed to open. Time to get up in the air. She had waited until now as she knew the roar of the engines would draw attention. Rita checked the fuel. It was about a quarter full. That would certainly be enough to get them sky bound and through the portal, but she suddenly realized she didn't know how to get back home!

Well, she thought, *nobody lives forever. Guess I'll see Mel again sooner than I thought.*

Turning the plane around, Rita looked at the open field and took a deep breath. "Hang on to your hat!" she called, then gunned the plane forward. Speed was critical as the makeshift runway was short, provided little margin for error. The plane zoomed forward, and she pulled back the stick at just the right moment sending it over the farmhouses and into the sky.

Rita consulted her watch. Two minutes before the rip in the sky appeared. Her plan was to linger around where Mr. Abbot said it was going to be, then race into the hole when it opened. The expression "man plans, God laughs" came to mind as the air exploded not a dozen yards away from them. Rita looked down to see a cadre of soldiers standing next to cannons in the courtyard. King Kohler was in their midst.

"Fire!" the king screamed, and fire they did. "Bring them down!"

"They're shooting at us!" Ivan cried.

Rita said nothing as she concentrated on her flying. She banked the plane to the side to avoid being hit. Normally, she would have either returned the fire or fled, but she had to stay up there and wait for the hole to open.

Twisting and turning, the Guardsman avoided being hit time and again. Ivan made retching noises. "Don't you dare dirty my plane!" she snapped, glad to have something to take her mind off what could be their impending death.

Rita was just banking away from a missile when shimmering lights appeared due east of her. The lights flashed on and off, forming a straight line up and down. Those on the ground must also have been mesmerized by them as the shelling stopped. There was a tearing sound and the lights pulled apart revealing a dark void.

"Here we go!" Rita shouted, more to herself than to Ivan. She turned the plane sideways, lining it up with the opening. There was little room to spare, and Radio Rita held her breath as she flew into the hole!

What happened next was one of the weirdest experiences of her life. All went dark and there was no sound of any kind. Rita felt as though her body had turned inside out. There was no up, no down, no left or right; no directional of any kind. There was only a sense of being, but without any accompanying feelings.

An untold time later, Rita felt her senses slowly returning. Her eyesight and hearing came first and soon after she was once more able to control her body. The first thing that struck her was that it was now night and, judging by the trees losing their leaves, autumn. There were also no mountains, no colorful houses, and no kingdom. What was below were trees and ivy-covered buildings in a semi-suburban area.

"I can't believe it! We're in Princeton, New Jersey," Ivan said excitedly. "Princeton University is where Kohler went to school in the early nineteen twenties."

Rita also found it hard to believe they had gone back in time and space, but her eyes told her it was real. She would think more on that later. Right now she had to land and quickly. If anyone saw their plane, which was way ahead of anything they had in those days, there would be questions she couldn't answer. Luckily, there was an empty lot nearby. Rita cut the engines and landed. Then they got out of the plane, covered it, and began walking into town toward a situation they had no clue about.

Ivan stopped as they passed under a streetlamp. Rita turned to see him looking down at himself. A smile played over his face. "Hey, look at me!"

Rita knew why he was so happy. "Your color is back." That was a good thing as she didn't know how they would have otherwise explained his black and white condition. "I guess since the dimension door hasn't been opened, the beings there don't have a hold on you."

Ivan stretched his muscles, then wrapped his arms around himself in a hug. "I can't tell you how good this feels. I forgot what it was like to be normal." A tear came to his eye. His next words were whispered. "I forgot what it was like to be human."

Rita smiled back, then something attracted her attention. Next to a bench was a garbage can on top of which was a newspaper. It was a copy of the New York Times which Rita fished out. They sat down and she peered through the paper.

"Okay, hard to believe, but since this seems to be yesterday's paper, today is May eleventh of nineteen twenty-one. Tell me what you know about Kohler being here." He was silent for a moment, still basking in his being whole again. "Ivan?"

Ivan looked at her blankly, then shook his head as if coming out of a dream. "Yes, yes, give me a moment," he said and composed himself. "Kohler was sent by his father to attend a United States university not only to get the best education possible, but also to learn the ways of Americans. In May of this year, he attended a lecture series here which helped him come up with his theory of how to open the bridge to that colorless dimension."

"What?" Rita questioned. "They couldn't have been giving a lecture on that."

"No," Ivan elaborated. "The story goes that Princeton sponsored a lecture on physics which opened King Kohler's mind to the ideas from which he came up with the dimension opening portal. The lectures were given by a visiting physicist by the name of Albert Einstein."

"Einstein?" Rita had flown Einstein on a clandestine mission to Germany to recruit a young scientist by the name of Werner Von Braun.

"Yes, do you know him?"

"I…" she began, then stopped as she realized that her meeting with Einstein was still in the future. If they met now, he would not know her. "I've heard of him."

Ivan nodded. "If I remember correctly, this morning Einstein will be taking an early morning walk before his lecture. Prince Kohler, out for a morning constitutional, will run into him by happenstance. The prince gives Einstein some ideas that aids the physicist with his work, and they become friends."

Rita did her best not to laugh. Kohler may have stopped and spoken to the genius, but there was no way that he gave Einstein ideas. Kohler may have been smart, but Einstein, well, Einstein was Einstein.

Ivan looked at his watch. "If you're right about what day it is, then that meeting should be happening soon as Einstein walked very early." He began to scan the area. "I remember some of these surroundings from pictures of Kohler's autobiography we were forced to memorize. I think we go toward the buildings."

They walked a bit before Ivan stopped and pointed down a path coming from off campus. "Look!" Up ahead was a man in his forties with long hair. He wore a dark cloak and a green knitted tie. Rita smiled upon seeing a younger version of the man she had (would have) such a fantastic adventure with one day.

"Einstein," she whispered.

"And look who's coming toward him from the opposite way," Ivan pointed.

Rita followed his directions to see a youthful, skinnier version of King Kohler headed for the physicist. The way he purposely walked toward the physicist showed this meeting was no accident. He was purposely seeking Einstein out.

"What now?" Ivan asked her.

"Let's get behind those trees over there and watch what happens. Hopefully, we'll figure out what we must do to keep your awful future from happening," Rita said wishing that Mr. Abbot was there.

Ivan nodded and the two of them went to the small, treed area. Pretending to talk to each other, Rita and Ivan looked on as Prince Kohler came up to Einstein, getting directly in his path. The physicist, occupied with his thoughts, just nodded to Kohler and walked around him. Rita saw the future king's face grow angry and he once again jogged over to stand in the smaller man's way. This time when Einstein moved to get past, Kohler didn't let him. The pair began to talk and, although Rita could hear what was going on, she didn't understand as they were speaking in German.

"I wish I knew what they were saying," she groaned.

"I do," Ivan said. "Besides our own language and English, Kohler makes all of us understand German, French and Spanish."

Rita thought that a good thing amongst all the bad Kohler did, but it was one against many. "Tell me what's going on," she said, and Ivan did.

"Kohler is telling Einstein how much he admires him. Einstein is saying thanks and now Kohler is explaining some physics to him. It is very complicated." Ivan translated. Rita got ready to see Einstein beg off, but the physicist listened intently to every word the other had to say.

"Keep listening," Rita said, but she didn't need a translator to understand what occurred next. When Kohler finished, he looked at Einstein triumphantly. The physicist smiled and started to speak, the tone of his words showed he was praising the other. Kohler puffed up accordingly. But then Einstein's smile faded, and he took out pencil and notepad and began to write, explaining what he was writing as he did.

Every pen stroke and every word from the physicist caused Kohler's smile to fade and he began to turn red. As Einstein continued, the prince's embarrassment changed to anger. The physicist didn't seem to notice as he was too wrapped up in what he was saying and writing. Suddenly, the prince let out an animalistic snarl. Rita's hair stood on end, and she tensed, ready to defend her future friend should Kohler attack him.

"Don't," Ivan said, taking her tightly by the arm.

She turned to him and saw his face looking grim. "Get your hand off me or lose it," she hissed.

"Sorry," Ivan said, putting his hands up in surrender.

Rita returned her attention to the unfolding scene but filed away what had just happened.

"I know you don't like what I am saying, but truth is truth," Einstein continued in English, not backing down or cowering from the other's anger. "And I know you to be smart enough to see where your mistakes were made whether you want to or not."

Although Einstein's words were kind, they did not calm the angry prince. "Do you know who I am? Do you have any idea what I am capable of?" Kohler roared. "I will be king one day! Ruler of all I survey!"

Einstein shrugged. "Physics works the same for king or commoner," he said. "What you are proposing is dangerous beyond your wildest dreams. I beg you, put that brilliant mind toward solving other problems. If you follow this path, you will surely regret…"

"Don't tell me what I will regret, you insignificant gnat!"

As Kohler raised his arm to strike Einstein, Rita raced forward. She thought

"Tell me what's going on," she said, and Ivan did.

she felt something grab at her from behind, but she was moving too fast for whatever it was to take hold. Before Kohler could bring his arm down, Rita was on him, tackling the future king with a flying leap. The prince was shocked at first, but then, showing surprising strength, threw her off. Both got to their feet at the same time.

"Get out of here, Professor Einstein," Rita said, as she stood between him and the seething Kohler. Her thought now was not on her mission, but on getting Einstein to safety as he had many great things ahead of him.

"I would, young lady, but we seem to be surrounded," the physicist said, and Rita realized that a septet of shiny metal automatons, heads numbered one through seven, appeared out of nowhere to form a circle around them.

Rita knew these were the machines that Kohler had invented and, except for number seven, did not last into her time. She also knew how dangerous they were, and that Kohler must have already invented the invisibility device that Mr. Abbot had/would use in their escape. As in the cell, the septet began to whir, a trio of blades popping out of them and spinning menacingly.

"Now who will regret today?" Kohler laughed and, at a nod, the deadly machines began to inch closer.

"I only had enough of their power source to make seven, but each model's better than the one before," Kohler continued. "I'm sure you'll both agree they are a stunning achievement."

"Listen to me, Kohler!" Rita saw no other choice than to reveal the future to him. "When you open the dimensional portal, you unleash deadly forces that you cannot control."

Kohler eyed her suspiciously. "Why should I believe that?" he asked while the killing machines moved closer.

"Because I'm from the future; 1939 to be exact," she admitted. "I've seen the mess you've made of your country and maybe even the world."

"This is what I warned would happen if you tampered with forces beyond your comprehension," Einstein said, not batting an eye over the idea that Rita was from the future.

"I invented a time machine?" Kohler asked.

"You did." Rita quickly came up with a plan. "The reason you did was to send me to warn your past self about the terrible things that will happen if you open that doorway."

Kohler motioned and the automatons stopped their forward progress. "Perhaps," he said, "and perhaps not. If I sent someone into the past, why didn't I send myself?"

Einstein handled that question. "Because you knew there would be severe consequences if you were in two places at once."

"Quite so." Kohler rubbed his chin. "I also know I would have given whoever was going back in time a code word which would let me believe them. So what's the word?"

'Uh-oh,' Rita mumbled to herself. "Swordfish?"

Kohler smiled at her. "Wrong," he hissed, then looked toward his deadly machines. "Automatons, on my command, kill…"

"Stop!" a voice cried. "She might not know the code word, but I do."

Ivan came out from behind the trees he and Rita had previously hidden in. Kohler quickly had number seven break rank to stand between himself and Ivan. The other six closed the circle behind him. The once pale man walked forward, automaton seven allowing him to come face to face with the future king.

"You work for Kohler?" Rita said in disbelief.

"He threatened to kill my family," Ivan said sadly. "I had no choice."

As Ivan leaned forward and said something softly to Kohler, Rita realized she had been set up. Ivan's paint crew were the only people out in the streets of Belakoya because Kohler wanted her to meet him and hear his phony tale of woe. Rita was allowed to escape because Kohler needed her to take his agent into the past. That also accounted for why Ivan had knocked out Mr. Abbot. And Kohler's missiles had missed her so she would think he didn't want her to go to the past when he really did.

But why had Kohler gone to all this trouble?

"You *are* from the future!" Kohler laughed and pounded Ivan on the back. Ivan recoiled under his liege's touch. "I am genius beyond my wildest dreams! Now what message do you have from my future self?"

"I've been sent to tell you not to go through with the dimensional opening," Ivan explained. "What these two have told you is true."

Rita's eyes went wide. Kohler wouldn't have sent back Ivan to warn himself not to open the doorway. He was too narcissistic to admit he had made a mistake, especially to himself. Could it be that Ivan was on her side now?

"I see. Thank you for telling me." The prince put out his hand and Ivan, a slight smile on his face, shook it. But as they grabbed hands, Kohler whirled his future subject around, pinning his arm behind him. While Ivan squirmed in pain, Kohler reached inside the other's jacket and pulled out a large rock which he threw on the ground.

"Really? Were you going to use this on me?" Kohler said, then dug deeper in the struggling man's pockets and took out an envelope emblazoned with his seal. Once he had it, he threw Ivan to the ground at the feet of number seven. "Kill him if he gets up."

The prince tore open the envelope, growing serious as he read the note inside. "Hmm… This letter explains why I shouldn't open the portal. It—"

Rita couldn't believe what she was hearing. "So you won't open it?"

Kohler glared at her. "It also tells how to fix the problem that lets the other dimension invade us. So now, we are going to not only open it, but conquer their world and enslave them."

"Preposterous," Einstein said.

"See for yourself. I've already memorized it." Kohler crumbled the paper and threw it into the circle. Rita ventured forward to retrieve it, then smoothed it out and handed the note to Einstein.

"Well?" Kohler asked. "Are you dazzled by my brilliance?"

The physicist sighed as he looked up from the note. "This is even more dangerous than what you originally proposed. If you—"

"I'll have no more of your jealousy!" Kohler interrupted. "I'm going to do whatever I want, and after I take over that other dimension, I will take over our world as well! And there is nothing you can do to stop me!"

Just then, some early morning walkers came into view. "Help!" Einstein cried, but they kept going. "Help!"

"Scream all you want," Kohler laughed. "I have employed a device of my own making that bends light and sound waves. They cannot hear you no matter how loud you yell."

Einstein gave Kohler a disappointed look. "What?" Kohler asked.

"I am thinking how you don't deserve your genius," the physicist said.

The prince's face grew red. "I will accomplish more than you ever will," he snapped. "It's too bad none of you will be around to see it."

Kohler nodded to his machines, which began to move toward them, the air filled with the sounds of the whirring blades. For some time now, Rita wondered when she died if she would go to her eternal reward or become a ghost like Mel. It seemed she was about to find…

Mel!

"I've got an idea," Rita said to Einstein. "Give me your coat, quickly!"

Einstein did so, and Rita wrapped it around her hands. Letting out a scream, she barreled forward, knocking over the nearest automaton. The blades inflicted some damage to her upper arms and body, but Einstein's coat protected her from how bad it could have been. Continuing forward, she slammed into number seven, pushing it to the ground, where it lay on its back, arm blades snapping about.

"You're only prolonging the inevitable," Kohler said and two of the killing machines left the circle to come for her. "Did you really think you could get the better of me?"

"It's not you I need to get the better of," she said, then turned her attention to Ivan. "Destroy number seven! It's our only hope!"

Kohler scoffed. "Even if that simpleton could destroy my creation, it wouldn't do you any good. Any one of the others is more than capable of handling all three of you!"

Ivan looked at Rita who was not doing well fending off the two robots. The pilot was suffering cuts to her whole body, and it was only a matter of time before a lethal blow landed. Ivan switched his gaze from her to Kohler. Anger welled up inside him as he stared at the tyrant who had threatened his family and forced him to endure such terrible pain. Picking up the rock he had meant to strike Kohler with, Ivan jumped inside the fallen machine's defenses and began to pound away at number seven's body and head. The blades cut Ivan hard and deep, but he kept going until the machine was bashed in and the blades stopped spinning.

"I did it!" Ivan said, grinning through his agony. "I…" His words trailed off as his future king kicked him in the face.

"You did nothing," Kohler laughed. "With what I'm going to accomplish…"

He continued talking, but Rita wasn't listening. As she fended off her attackers, she saw something new had entered the scene. Shimmering into existence about five feet from her was a white, ghostly shape. Mel.

Her plan had worked!

But would it be enough?

"Where am I?" he asked. Mel's eyes narrowed as he saw Rita covered with blood, trying to fend off the machines. "Rita! Who did this to you?"

He went toward her, but she shook her head. "No time for explanations!" she roared. "Possess Kohler!"

"Really?" Mel asked. "You believe I can do it?"

"Just do it!" she roared.

"Done!" Mel's ghostly form whipped through the air and plunged into the still pontificating prince. Kohler suddenly went still, a look of shock spreading across his face. The machines also stopped moving. Rita, Einstein, and Ivan all came to stand before the now motionless Prince Kohler.

"You have a ghost in your employ?" Einstein asked. Rita nodded.

"I don't get it," Ivan stated.

"Number seven imprisoned Mel, the ghost, years from now. Your breaking the machine kept that from happening," Radio Rita explained. "I figured that would mean his showing up here which is where he otherwise would have been."

"One of many possible outcomes but, luckily, it worked," Einstein stated. "However, the fact you remain here shows that Kohler will still open the dimensional door or commit some other atrocious act. If he didn't, you would have had no need to come here and would vanish from this era."

"Whatever you plan on doing, make it quick!" Mel, using Kohler's mouth, said. "I don't know how long I can hold him."

While Rita was realizing she hadn't planned anything other than stopping the attack on them, Ivan went into action. He grabbed the rock he had beaten number seven with and leapt forward. "Die like a dog!" Ivan roared and swung it toward his king. But his rock filled hand stopped inches from Kohler's face and Ivan screamed in pain. "Ow!"

"I activated my personal force after that first attack on my personage," Kohler said, regaining control of his mouth. "Your ghost's resolve is waning. In moments I will be free and make you all wish you'd never been born!"

Einstein pulled Rita down so he could whisper in her ear. "Can you speak to your ghost with your mind?" he asked. Rita nodded. "Have him make Kohler hold his breath."

Rita looked at him puzzled. "What will that do?"

"If the ghost can take over Kohler's autonomous nervous system, we can deprive that magnificent, yet flawed, brain of oxygen thereby destroying enough cells to keep him from ever being a threat," the physicist explained.

Rita turned white. "Won't that kill him?"

Einstein shook his head. "No, but he will never be the same. Arguably, what we are doing is worse than killing him, but I see no other way."

Rita didn't either. She turned her mind to the ghost. "*Have Kohler hold his breath.*"

The ghost did as directed and the future king stopped breathing. Kohler, realizing what they were doing, fought hard against Mel, his body shaking with the struggle. Although Mel was no quitter, Rita could see he wasn't going to beat Kohler. The future king was just too strong for him.

"He can't hold on!" Rita said to Einstein.

"Use your link with the ghost to send your mind into his to help him," the physicist told her.

"Can I do that?"

Einstein shrugged. "Why not?"

Rita shut her eyes and concentrated like never before. One second later, she found herself torn from her body and in a dark, alien landscape, blue and red lightning bolts sailing across the sky. A hundred yards away, Rita saw three people engaged in mortal combat. It was Mel and Kohler...and another Kohler! Mel had one Kohler in a headlock, while the second Kohler beat away at him.

Every time the second Kohler landed a punch, pieces of Mel flew off into oblivion.

Rita ran between the Kohlers, pushing the attacking version back so he could no longer get to Mel. Her Kohler, more animal than human, hissed and came forward in a bull run. She was about to punch him, when he changed directions and swept out his leg, knocking her to the ground. Although dazed, Rita reached out and grabbed his ankle, causing him to fall before he could get to the struggling pair. Quickly, Rita rolled on top of him and held on with every fiber of her being. Though the future king furiously bucked and kicked, he could not get free. His motions grew weaker with each passing second, until he barely moved.

"I'll... be... ba—" his mind whispered.

"No, you won't," she interrupted, then abruptly found herself returned to her physical body. Kohler stood in front of her, his mouth hanging open, his gaze unfocused. "We did it!"

There was an exclamation of joy next to her. "Then my family and country are finally free!" a smiling Ivan said. "Thank you, Rita, thank you!" He was still smiling when he vanished.

Rita looked around, any feeling of accomplishment fading away when she couldn't find the ghost. She turned to Einstein. "Where's Mel?"

"He isn't here?" Einstein asked. Rita had forgotten that he couldn't see him.

"No," she said, remembering how Kohler's blows had cut him to pieces. Could his heroic act have allowed him his final reward? She grew dizzy at the thought, then realized that she too was fading away.

"Quickly!" Einstein said, grasping her by the shoulders. "Tell me everything that has brought us to this point so I can make sure it never happens again!"

Rita gathered what little strength she had left and rapidly told Einstein what had happened starting with the foreign visitor to her office, to her travelling through time. A thought occurred to her as she finished and saw her body growing insubstantial.

"Where am I going?" she whispered.

The physicist shrugged. "The changing of time could send you anywhere and affect anything and everything," he told her, then his tone turned warm. "You saved the world, Rita, and even if nobody else remembers..."

Then his words vanished into the ether, and so did she.

Radio Rita looked up from the next day's flight plans, a feeling of déjà vu sweeping over her. She glanced out the window of her office at the almost completed LaGuardia airport. There was nobody there. She went to the door and looked out. Still nobody.

'Who were you expecting?' she asked herself, but she knew. Other pilots had told about a foreign man who had come to their offices looking for someone to deliver a package to King Kohler of Belakoya. Big money had been offered, but all turned it down knowing how eccentric that king was and how dangerous the route to his kingdom. Rita might have agreed to take on the delivery; not because of the money, but because the subject of King Kohler had always fascinated her.

Rita had read that Kohler had been brilliant once, coming across the ocean to attend Princeton University. He'd been top of the class until a mysterious early morning accident took away that brilliance leaving the then prince with a damaged mindset. Kohler had been found by Albert Einstein, the brilliant inventor of the invisible shield that her country used to send operatives to Germany, Italy and Japan to take-out would-be dictators.

Rita was friends with Einstein, having flown him around the country many times as the physicist always asked for her. Each time they flew, Rita questioned him over the Kohler incident, something inside her needing to know what happened. But each ask brought the same enigmatic answer of 'it's not time' which made Rita… Her heartbeat bumped up as she heard someone at her door.

The portal opened to reveal, not the foreign man, but her partner Mel Esposito. Mel was prematurely white-haired and pale. Rita blamed herself for that. Mel was a former gangster who blew the whistle on fellow mobsters for immunity. Rita was assigned to fly him to a safehouse, but they'd been intercepted by Mel's former comrades. Rita had gotten him to safety, but the perilous journey had turned Mel's hair white, and his skin ghostly. Afterwards, Mel had vowed to be Rita's bodyguard.

"Didn't you already leave for the day?" she asked.

Mel shrugged. "Yeah, but I got this weird feeling I should be here, so here I am. Took me longer than expected as only the seven line was running and you know I won't take it. Had to hail a cab."

"I never understood your fear of the number seven."

"Me neither," Mel shrugged, then snapped his fingers. "Oh, I heard the government arrested that guy from Belakoya who was soliciting pilots. Word is that he was a—"

They were interrupted by a knock at the door which opened to reveal a man familiar to both.

"Professor Einstein!" Rita exclaimed as the famous physicist entered. "To what do we owe the pleasure?"

Einstein smiled at them bittersweetly. "I'm here because it's finally time."

Rita felt her pulse pound. "Time to tell about that morning at Princeton University?"

"Yes. Because today's the day that the end of the world would have started but didn't because of the two of you."

Mel and Rita looked at each other and then at the physicist. "This I got to hear!" Mel said.

"Yes, Professor Einstein," Rita said, feeling that the void from not knowing the answer was about to be filled, "do tell."

And Einstein did.

THE END

The Seversky 2PA is the two-seat version of the single seat P-35 model manufactured by the Seversky Company, which was later reformed under the name Republic Aviation. Before World War 2 hostilities with Japan, 20 planes were sold to that country. In June 1940, the United States government ordered an embargo on the sale of U.S. made aircraft to all foreign countries except Britain. Sweden had received two aircraft of their order, and the remaining 50 were sold to the United States Army Air Corps and designated the AT-12 Guardsman. It is unlikely that any AT-12 served as an advanced trainer, however, as most were allocated during World War 2 to USAAC base commanding officers as fast transport aircraft.

Jumping Off the Deep End

Five foot nine, red hair, a pilot and...*go!*

That's pretty much the instructions we were given to create a story about Radio Rita and that was good enough for me!

I wanted to start with a bang; an aerial battle to showcase my Rita's skills, fearlessness, and ingenuity against impossible odds. Should she have a co-pilot? That was a tough one. While I didn't want too many characters, I like to propel the story (and explain the backstory) through dialogue rather than flashbacks. I opted for a co-pilot, Mel, but that seemed too ordinary. I know! Why not make him a ghost; one that may, or may not, be a figment of Rita's imagination. I honestly didn't know what he was until the end when circumstances forced me to make that decision.

Now they needed a task. As the story is set just before the beginning of World War II with much of Europe in unrest, I decided the conflict should take place there. I made up a nation rather than setting it in a real one as that would allow me to compose my own history. When I was thinking of names for it, a surprising number of what I came up with were actual places! Who knew naming a country was so hard?

As there were still monarchies in Europe at the time, mine could be one and the king of the country the villain. For the king's name. I wanted something easy to remember. The first name I thought of was Old King Cole. With a little tweaking, and staring at my sink faucet, he became King Kohler. Now to his personality. I started out having him a buffoon but couldn't figure how he would stay in power. A Facebook friend had recently posted about the movie *The Great Race* where Jack Lemon played both an evil genius and a silly monarch. I decided to mix the two together, although the silly part was a smokescreen.

An evil genius should have an evil plan, but Kohler's was simple; he wanted to turn his little kingdom into a big kingdom. It was the execution of that plan that was complex. Since Kohler could use the wealth of his country to do anything and he was super intelligent, I needed something that would show his ingenuity, but be a poor choice on his part. I came up with his going into another dimension, but not being prepared for what he would find there. The idea of paint being used to hold them off came from some waterproof painting I was doing.

At first, Ivan was just a tragic character introduced to show Kohler's uncaring. Mr. Abbot was originally to go through time with Rita, but I wanted to show Kohler's intelligence and having him prepared for Abbot's treachery would do that. So Ivan became Kohler's agent in the kings plan to stop the dimensional beings. But how would he do that? I didn't know; I had written myself into a corner. Then it occurred to me that Kohler himself could change the problem. He could invent a time machine allowing him to open the portal without the trouble that ensued.

But where in Kohler's lifetime should I have them go? I had a throwaway line about Kohler bragging in his autobiography that he was so smart he taught Einstein a thing or two. Doing some quick research, I found that Einstein gave a series of lectures at Princeton University in May of 1921 so that's where I set the time machine to take Rita and Ivan. I figured Kohler would have guards, but ones of his own making so I came up with the automatons.

Once Kohler met Einstein and trapped him, Rita and Ivan, I realized I had two problems. One, I didn't know how to get them out of Kohler's trap and two, I had completely forgotten about Mel. To solve both problems, I had an automaton capture Mel in the jail cell (which accounted for his disappearance in the story) and, with some time manipulation, I had him reappear to save the trio by taking over Kohler's body. As Mel had not shown that ability before, I had to go back and write in a few instances of him previously showing that power. At first, I had Mel defeat Kohler, but Rita was the star so I changed that to her beating Kohler in a duel of minds.

And that was the end.

But it wasn't.

The story felt incomplete as I wanted to know what happened to Rita and Mel after they got rid of Kohler. I spent a while figuring that out. With Kohler's brainpower diminished at Princeton, he never hired Rita to come to his country therefore everything else was moot. However changing history changes history. Mel was never killed, so he never became a ghost although his countenance was now pale and ghostly. He was also scared of the number seven (he wouldn't take the seven train) as that was the number of the surviving automaton who imprisoned him in the other reality. Even though Rita didn't remember the whole affair, something in the back of her mind nagged her about it. I wanted it to seem that it might have been a dream. That is shattered by Einstein arriving and finally being able to tell the story about what happened that she could not remember.

So it was real, but it wasn't…and that was exactly what I wanted.

GLEN HELD - Born on a Monday, Glen grew up in the legendary borough of Brooklyn before moving to Long Island where culture shock set in. Fear not; our boy survived (barely) middle class suburbia. College at Stony Brook University followed, wherein he unwisely majored in Psychology & English. Falling into an alternate dimension, Glen turned his hand to government work where he was paroled (retired) after a thirty-year sentence.

Nowadays, Glen still lives on Long Island—with his wife and Eddie the Dog—and is very, very proud of his children.

Glen is the author of the accliamed pulp team-up *The Devil You Know* and the Best Pulp pNovel nominated *Legends in the Earth.*

Follow Glen on Facebook (Glen Held) and/or the pretentiously named handsomegh at Instagram.

Radio Rita and the Malvor Report

by Samantha Lienhard

1944

Rita crept through the underbrush. She'd got the information she needed, and now she needed to get back to the plane she'd hidden not far away. Easier said than done. The Germans had swarmed the area since her arrival. At least the activity appeared unrelated to her presence, but that wouldn't matter if she got caught. While she had a handgun at her side, she didn't favor her odds if it turned into a firefight.

Infiltrating the lab to steal the research data had been tricky, but this was supposed to be the easy part. Next time Simmons sent her on a mission like this, she'd be sure to plan a strategy for the worst-case scenario.

She hid in the bushes and turned on her radio. Maybe she could get an idea of the situation if she picked up the right communications.

Static crackled, and then a distorted voice broke through. "…anyone… …me? …there? …Can't… …longer!"

Well, that sure wasn't a German, not unless this was an elaborate trick meant to bait out any Allied operatives in the area—which, considering her infiltration of the lab still hadn't been detected by the time she left, would be an impressive bit of planning. On the other hand, no one from the Allies was supposed to be here besides her. This number of enemy soldiers wasn't supposed to be here *either*, though, so their intelligence might have balled this up entirely.

She gritted her teeth. Head straight back with the stolen documents like Simmons had instructed, or try to help the distressed man on the radio?

There really was only one answer. Unless it looked so dangerous that the entire mission would be placed in jeopardy, she couldn't leave someone in danger. And since no one knew she was there, she liked her odds.

Of course, it would help if the man stopped shouting on an unencrypted channel in enemy territory. But she'd still take these odds.

Rita checked the radio again and began trying to track the signal.

At last, she reached a tiny shack, where a gray-haired man cowered behind a backpack nearly as large as he was. He lifted a gun in trembling hands and pointed it at her. "D-Don't come any closer!"

"Relax," she said, "I'm on your side."

He slowly lowered the gun and blinked at her from his hiding place like an old, spindly owl. "Why… you're a girl!"

"Thanks," she said dryly. "Now that we're past your observational skills, who in blazes are you and why are you behind enemy lines?"

His shoulders slumped. "My name is Thomas Malvor; I'm a scientist. Our plane went off course and was shot down…" He shuddered and covered his face. "I'm the only one who made it out of the wreckage. I took the pilot's gun and hid, but I really don't know what I'm doing…"

"You held out long enough for a rescue. That's all that matters." She held out her hand. "I'm on my way out of here myself, so you can hitch a ride with me."

He took her hand and got to his feet. "Oh thank you, thank you so much!"

"Stay behind me and keep a low profile," she said. "There's a lot more enemies in this area than I expected, and we don't want to draw any unnecessary attention."

He nodded, and she led the way to the door.

Outside, things still looked relatively peaceful for now. Rita glanced from side to side, then dropped into a crouch. The scientist followed her lead.

"I've heard about you WACs," he said behind her as they snuck away from the shack. "To be honest, I had my doubts, but not now that you saved my life!"

"I'm technically not with the Women's Army Corps anymore," she said. "I work directly for the government now. More importantly, when I said we shouldn't draw unnecessary attention, that includes being as quiet as possible."

"Oh." He rubbed the back of his neck. "Sorry."

She shook her head. Scientists.

It took the better part of the afternoon, but they finally made it back to where she'd concealed her P-61 Black Widow fighter. Malvor's eyes lit up at the sight of the plane. "Why, this is one of the new night fighters, isn't it? Might I have a look at how the radar operates?"

"Go ahead," she said. "It's built for a crew anyway, and we've got a long flight ahead of us."

"I didn't even know the WAC had been issued planes like this!"

"Government agent," she said.

"Yes, yes, of course."

Considering how their interactions had gone so far, she'd lay odds he wouldn't actually remember that. Well, it didn't matter anyway. All she had to do was get him to safety. Unless Simmons decided to recruit him, their paths would likely never cross again.

10 years later…

"An escort mission, huh?" Rita folded her arms. "So all we need is this scientist brought safely back here?"

She had arrived at her boss's office shortly after receiving his message at the radio station that morning. The code he'd used was one of their simplest, a request for her to report to him as soon as possible. Despite the relaxing atmosphere of the room, with artwork hanging on the walls and a prototype video screen showing a simulated view of the streets above, the urgency in his voice kept her alert.

"It is of the utmost importance." Simmons looked gravely serious. A document sat in front of him on his mahogany desk, its contents apparently related to the matter at hand. "Thomas Malvor's research into radar and missile guidance technology, informally dubbed the Malvor Report, will be invaluable to our country. He says it's all contained within his head, with nothing written down. Therefore, it's imperative that we get him to Washington as quickly as possible. He has reported numerous attempts on his life already."

"Well," Rita said, "that answers my next question. I was about to ask why he can't come here on his own. Who's after him?"

"To the best of our knowledge, multiple countries are involved, as well as some private corporations."

Of course. It could never be something simple.

Yet for them, this was an ordinary day's work. Another assignment, another job, the sort she had gotten used to in the years since she'd joined the Hand of the Law to continue her work for Simmons even after the war ended.

Although the halls outside the office were bustling with activity as agents went about their business and scientists worked on their latest developments, most people didn't know any of it existed at all. To the people walking on the streets above, it must seem unfathomable that such activity occurred deep beneath the building known to the public only as Reports and Accounting.

Behind that façade, the Hand of the Law did its job to prevent threats that might otherwise threaten the country or even the world—and the Malvor Report had been deemed one of them.

"Malvor…" Rita frowned. "That name sounds familiar."

"It should be. It's why I chose you for this assignment."

She'd wondered if there was a specific reason for her selection. At 5'8, with flaming red hair, her style of undercover work usually involved drawing attention to herself with a false story to provide cover for other parts of the mission, but this didn't sound like that sort of job. Her knowledge of computers gave her an edge in certain missions, yet that didn't seem to be involved here either.

While she had the combat skills to protect herself and anyone she was escorting, they had many agents more capable in those areas, as well.

"Do you recall a mission during the war when you rescued a scientist who had been trapped behind enemy lines?" Simmons asked.

The name clicked. She snapped her fingers. "Thomas Malvor, of course!" After ten years, the memory of that encounter had faded. She blinked. "Wait, *he's* the one who needs an escort?"

"Precisely. He was grateful to you at the time, so it is my belief that having you present will be of inestimable importance when it comes to convincing him to work with us."

Compared to all the other missions Rita had handled during the war and later on as part of the Hand, Malvor's rescue was a minor incident, but for him, it must have been one of the most important days of his life. Given his age and temperament, she had expected him to live out the rest of his days without any drama, but apparently not.

"You'd better catch me up to speed on Malvor," she said. "Wasn't he already working for the government?"

"Not quite. During the war, Malvor was part of a private company contracted to assist the military. Afterwards, he left the company in order to pursue private research. He's done occasional stints with other companies or the military over the years, but has remained unattached."

Rita folded her arms. "So he technically *could* sell his research to the highest bidder."

"Could, but likely won't. He contacted us asking for help, after all."

"All right. I'll see what I can do."

"Excellent. You'll be working with Edgar Grayson for this mission."

She winced. "Have I done something wrong?" Her last few jobs had been successful, the radio station fulfilled its role better than ever these days, and she didn't recall any recent altercations, except… "It was Jones, wasn't it? Look, I don't know how that cat got into his office, but I didn't have anything to do with it."

Simmons rolled his eyes and pinched the bridge of his nose. "Being assigned to work with Grayson is not a punishment."

"That is a matter of opinion."

Edgar Grayson was one of the premier agents with the Hand. He'd been there for longer than her, as he worked for Simmons before the war. He was experienced, capable, and reliable. He also had no sense of humor whatsoever.

"Why not Misha?" she asked. Her longtime partner Misha might be a grouch on occasion, but he had nothing on Grayson. Grayson could out-grump just about everyone she knew.

"Dr. Malvor is afraid of Russians due the incident in which you rescued him."

Rita furrowed her brow. "Sorry, did I lose track of something here? Russia was on our side during the war. Malvor was shot down by Nazis."

"Indeed. However, it would seem he can't tell the difference between German and Russian accents."

She raised her eyebrows. "You have to be joking."

No hint of amusement crossed his face. He was serious, then. Rita rubbed her forehead. *Scientists.* When she got Malvor back to safety all those years ago, he'd cheerfully repeated his newfound respect for the WAC. He must be one of those people whose brainpower was fully devoted to his work—the sort who could whip out a scientific achievement so impressive it had multiple governments gunning for him but couldn't remember his rescuer's occupation or distinguish between accents.

"All right," Rita said, "so Misha can't go on this mission. But why Grayson?"

"He is highly competent."

"We can't stand each other."

"You will have to put your personal differences aside for the sake of the mission."

Rita made a face.

Simmons ignored her reaction and continued with the briefing. "Malvor has currently taken refuge with Count Aleister Ravinton, a gentleman who claims to be descended from British nobility despite living in the midwestern United States. From the information we've been able to gather about him, he has only a single employee who attends to him and the mansion at which he resides, as he is a recluse."

"How did Malvor wrangle himself an invitation, then?"

"It seems they were old classmates, so Ravinton offered him safe harbor due to the threats on his life."

"Is Ravinton likely to cause problems for us?"

"All our information suggests Malvor is with him by choice, so he shouldn't object to his guest leaving."

That made things considerably simpler.

"There is one thing you should be aware of, however."

Something in his voice told her he was about to destroy her illusions of an easy, straightforward job. "What is it?"

"Dr. Malvor's request for aid came three days ago." His expression grew grim. "We'd hoped to gather more information about the organizations targeting him before we sent someone in, but we have been unable to contact him since then. Nor have we been able to get in touch with Ravinton."

"So there's a chance that our enemies have already made a move."

"Or that Ravinton cannot be trusted."

She sighed and shook her head. "I suppose it's too much to hope that a bad storm simply knocked out the phone lines."

Grayson was waiting for her in the lab with the scientists with his usual dour expression. "I understand we'll be working together." He spoke in the morose tones of a man about to attend his own funeral.

She folded her arms. "Don't sound so happy about it."

"I hope you intend to take this job seriously."

"I take all my jobs seriously."

Tall enough that even Rita needed to look up at him, Grayson had a powerful build and chiseled features that would be considered handsome if he wasn't *frowning* all the time. She'd swear his face was stuck that way. His perpetual frown deepened further. "Forgive me if my impression of you has been the opposite."

"Lovely. I'd tell you my impression of you, but I try not to use that sort of language."

Their bickering was disrupted by the arrival of Dr. James, one of the Hand's top scientists. Either missing or ignoring the tension between them, he greeted them with a cheerful smile. "Ah, it's good that you're here. I've got some top-of-the-line tech for you today. Whatever you're dealing with out there, you'll be well-prepared."

"Glad to hear it," Rita said.

Over the next hour, they looked over the equipment they'd be taking with them for this assignment. Rita got a series of lockpicks disguised as an ornamental hairpiece and a custom alarm built into her bracelet, Grayson had a radio concealed within a wristwatch, and they each had a variety of other useful things they could carry unseen.

"Are you ready to go?" he asked, once they finished.

Rita rubbed her chin. One of her primary duties for the Hand was to manage their radio station and receive coded messages other agents sent in under the guise of song requests. However, Simmons had already assigned Will to watch over it in her absence. Ever since they crossed paths in that one mission, the kid had begun to help them out more and more, and she'd shown him the ropes of how to handle their secret radio messages. The station should be in good hands, and she'd be able to check in with him on their way to the hangar anyway.

That only left letting Misha know that she was going, but—

Speak of the devil, the lab door opened and Misha stepped inside. He walked toward them with folded arms. "I heard you've got a new assignment without me."

"Yep. Our charge is afraid of European accents, so I've been partnered with Mr. No Fun himself."

"I can hear you, you know," Grayson said.

"That's why I said it."

He scowled.

"Try not to blow anything up," Misha said.

Rita narrowed her eyes and jabbed a finger at his chest. "Keep it up, and I won't say goodbye to you next time."

"We both know you will anyway."

"Sure, sure. Good luck with whatever work Simmons gives you while I'm gone. Maybe you'll be the one to blow something up this time."

Misha ignored her and looked at Grayson. "Watch out for her."

"As in protect her or beware of her?" he asked.

"Neither one is necessary," Rita said, at the same time Misha said, "Protect."

Grayson shook his head. "Strange, I expected the opposite."

Rita shrugged. "Fine, if that's how you want it, I promise I'll protect you."

"No, I meant—"

"You don't have to worry about a thing!" She pumped her fist into the air. "Let them throw whatever they want at us; I can handle it all."

"I certainly don't need *your* protection."

Misha sighed. "Are you two really going to be all right on that long flight together?"

"Flight?" Grayson asked.

"Sure, how did you think we were getting there?" Rita asked. "This Ravinton guy lives in the middle of nowhere. We have to fly."

"Absolutely not." Grayson's frown deepened into a scowl. "If you think I'm going to get into a modified fighter plane flown by *you* of all people—"

"I happen to be an excellent pilot, and I have the military commendations to prove it. I'll get us there in one piece, no worries."

"You say that, yet I cannot shake this fear that flying with you will result in me being dumped into the ocean."

"We're not even flying over the ocean for this mission. Besides, if that happened, it would be fully intentional."

"That is not a point in your favor."

Misha shook his head. "I hope Simmons knows what he's doing, pairing up the two of you."

Rita loved her modified F-94 Starfire. It filled her with nostalgia for when she first started flying, and the advanced modifications meant it had tech higher than she ever dreamed of back in those days. The only thing that made her happier than getting into the cockpit was the look on Grayson's face as he got into the second seat.

She pulled on her helmet and goggles, then guided the plane onto the runway in the secret underground hangar beneath the radio station. She cleared her throat. "Off we go, into the wild blue yonder—"

"Must you sing?" Grayson asked.

"Yes."

She had never, in fact, sung while taking off before, but it seemed like the sort of thing that would get under his skin for no good reason, so she continued to sing. By the time the plane took off from beneath the rocky outcropping that kept it hidden, she had finished all four verses and Grayson looked like he was on the brink of despair.

"So," she said once she caught her breath, "got any hobbies?"

Grayson glanced at her like he thought the question might be a trap.

She snapped her fingers. "I've got it. Brooding. Your hobby is brooding, isn't it?"

"Clearly yours is being insufferable."

"I've been told I'm charming."

"I highly doubt that."

"Actually, I'm normally much more agreeable. Something about you just brings out my urge to be annoying."

"Spare me."

"I'll try, if you try to act like a normal human in return. Seriously, what's your hobby? You must have something you like to do for fun."

"Reading."

"Anything good?"

"Yes."

Rita gave up.

For the rest of the flight, she ignored him. There was no point in making small talk when Grayson was as boring as she thought he was. Fortunately, he was also quiet, so she just pretended she was alone. There was nothing she enjoyed more than a private flight, even if the other seat was technically occupied.

At last, they reached their destination—an open, isolated field outside of the forest where Ravinton resided. The forest was vast and deep, the treetops completely hiding the mansion from view. Rita circled once to scout the area and then landed in the field.

"Told you I'd get us here in one piece," she said.

"Miracles do exist."

Rita got out of the plane, and Grayson followed. He reached into his pocket and pulled out a small bottle of pills, which he looked over carefully before returning it.

"Wait, are you sick?" she asked.

"As far as this mission is concerned, yes."

"I don't follow."

He folded his arms. "It's a strategy. If I take pills at regular intervals, anyone observing me will assume I have a condition that requires them. Depending on the situation, I can then use that misconception to feign illness, insist upon a break to take my medicine, fake a sudden attack, or otherwise gain an advantage."

"That's the most deranged plan I've ever heard," she said.

"I should have known you—"

"I like it."

"Suddenly, I have my doubts."

"No, really," she said. "It's unique, unexpected, and potentially quite useful. I always favor plans like that; it's why I had this bracelet made." She held up her arm to indicate the golden piece of jewelry around her wrist.

"Exactly what does your bracelet do?"

She pressed the hidden button on the edge of the bracelet. Several seconds passed in silence, and then the sound of church bells emanated from the secret speaker. The bells tolled three times and then stopped.

Grayson stared at her. "That's it?"

"It's more useful than you might think."

"I know I will regret asking this, but *how*?"

"Misha and I set up a coded system based on numbers. One means 'I'm here,' two means 'stay back,' three means 'move in now,' and so on. But if you shout a number out suddenly, people might get suspicious."

"So instead you use church bells, the most inconspicuous of sounds."

"Most people won't expect that to be a signal," she said.

"With good reason." Grayson scowled. "Everyone knows secret signals should be words that are worked naturally into conversation."

"Fine, fine… if I ever need you to play dead, I'll just say 'deranged.'"

"Please do not."

"What, you don't even like my codewords?"

"Personally, I'm starting to feel the ideal codeword on a mission with you is 'regret.'"

She laughed and shook her head. This was an intriguing piece of the puzzle called Edgar Grayson. Her prior impression of him had been that he was stodgy,

He reached into his pocket and pulled out a small bottle of pills...

no fun, and did everything completely by-the-books, but his medicine plan wasn't in any book she'd ever heard of. He must have come up with it himself.

"Still, two of out three," she said to herself.

"What?" Grayson asked.

"Never mind."

He snorted, but didn't press the point.

They gathered up their gear and equipment and headed toward the line of trees, where a dirt trail led into the depths. Once they crossed through, the treetops were so thick that they all but blocked out the light, like a canopy. Everything was thick and overgrown, with only glimpses of the trail visible beneath the grass and weeds.

"Well," Rita said, "this seems safe."

"Roads like this should be maintained to keep them in better condition."

"Is this really a road? I think even calling it a path is being generous."

The underbrush and pine needles crunched under their feet. Crickets chirped in the depths of the forest. Things darkened further with every step, until only the faintest hint of light made it through the trees.

"So the reclusive count lives all alone in a spooky forest with no sunlight," Rita observed. "Maybe he's a vampire."

"That's absurd."

She glanced up at Grayson, who stared straight ahead, near expressionless despite his complaint. "You should keep an open mind."

"This has nothing to do with how open my mind is."

"Don't you think it's a little funny that someone would live in a place like this?"

"He's a recluse. It's hardly unusual at all."

"You're thinking based on logic."

He glanced at her. "Dare I ask what *your* thinking is based on?"

"Atmosphere."

Grayson groaned and pinched the bridge of his nose. "I was a fool to think I could get something reasonable out of you."

"Shame, for a moment I thought you were almost human."

They continued walking in silence.

At least they weren't coming up on the recluse unawares. Word had been sent to Malvor before they lost contact that the Hand would send someone to escort him safely to Washington. If everything went well, he would be prepared to leave immediately. On the other hand, depending on exactly what the situation was, this could quickly turn into a rescue mission instead.

Wind whistled through the trees and rustled the underbrush. In the near darkness, every sound seemed exaggerated. Rita took a flashlight out of her purse and turned it on. The canopy of trees above them was so thick that it was nearly as dark as night. The beam from her flashlight cut through the darkness to illuminate the way in front of them.

Beside her, Grayson walked on, face fixed straight ahead, expression as serious as when they started. For him, it was just another job. Still, he could at least come up with a few jokes about the situation. She sighed.

"What?" he asked after a moment.

"Know any good jokes?"

Grayson said nothing. He looked like he regretted even asking.

They continued on in silence. The sooner they finished the job, the better.

At last, the trees ahead began to thin out to form a clearing in which an aged mansion was built. The building almost looked part of the forest itself, with the trees clustered close around it. Its dark wood had long since been overtaken with moss and creeping vines, which gave it an enchanted appearance.

A narrow path led up to the front door. Their footsteps crunched over gravel and pine needles as they made their way. Rita looked at the thick metal door knocker, then grabbed it and rapped the door.

The door opened, and an elderly man with white hair peered out. Dressed in black, he looked like he was some sort of butler, most likely the single staff member Simmons mentioned. He looked at the two of them. "Y-Yes?"

His nervousness made Rita go on alert. It could simply be that he was unused to dealing with visitors, but the circumstances meant it might be far more serious. She cleared her throat. "We're friends of Dr. Malvor. We sent word ahead that we would be coming."

The man slowly nodded. "Yes, yes… My master did mention that we would have more guests soon… and such capable guests too… Such a strange situation we've found ourselves in, after living in peace for so many years… Come in, come in…" Still mumbling under his breath, he backed away to let them inside.

Rita exchanged glances with Grayson, and they walked into the mansion.

The foyer was beautiful—or at least it would have been if it had proper lighting and looked like it had been cleaned in the past decade. Cobwebs strung from corner to corner did nothing to improve her impression of the place.

"Obviously haunted," she said under her breath.

Grayson glared at her.

The butler led them to the doors at the far end of the foyer and pushed them open onto an entrance hall that beat the foyer in grandeur thanks to a dazzling chandelier that cast sparkling lights down upon the marble floor, and a massive staircase that curled up to the second floor. This area looked to be better maintained, although there were still cobwebs in the highest corners.

A door across from the stairs opened, and a man stepped out. Tall, with black hair and a piercing blue-eyed gaze, and dressed in a blue silk smoking jacket, this had to be the mysterious Count Aleister Ravinton.

She gave her watch an idle glance. It was 7:00 in the evening. The sun would have set by now. The vampire theory remained on the table.

Grayson glared at her even though she hadn't said anything. Well, if he could sense her thoughts, he must secretly be thinking the same thing. She smirked at him, and he looked away with a deeper scowl.

"Good evening," the count said. "I am Count Aleistor Ravinton. I am happy to welcome my dear friend's guests to my manor."

He spoke clearly and precisely, all his words enunciated, like he came from another era. Rita checked off another box in her mental vampire checklist despite the tangible displeasure radiating from her partner, then cleared her throat and opened her mouth to speak.

Grayson spoke up before she could say a word. "We would like to see Dr. Malvor."

"Certainly, certainly. Bernard, tell Thomas that his guests are here."

The butler bowed and started up the stairs.

"Please," Ravinton said, "join me in the drawing room while we wait."

They followed the count through the door he'd come from, into the wide drawing room connected to the foyer. It had two couches as well as an armchair. Rita sat down on the couch, and Grayson sat next to her, stiff and straight as if at attention. The count settled into the armchair across from them and steepled his fingers as he regarded them.

"It is terrible, the danger that has befallen my old friend."

"Yes," Rita said, "it is."

"I assume you are accustomed to dealing with such dangers, if you are the ones who have been sent by the government."

"We will ensure no harm comes to him," Grayson said with a solemn nod.

"Don't worry about a thing." Rita shifted, and the movement caused a cloud of dust to erupt from the cushion. She coughed and waved away the dust.

"Forgive the state of the manor," Ravinton apologized. "Bernard is my only staff member, and he has trouble keeping up with the maintenance on his own, particularly now that he's gotten older."

"Why not hire someone else?" shc asked.

Ravinton folded his arms. "I enjoy my privacy."

Of course. Of course the man living in an isolated forest with hardly any sunlight would prefer to be holed up alone with a single butler who couldn't even get the job done. It was a miracle he had any employees at all. Bernard was probably the only person willing to even accept a job like this at the creepy mansion in the middle of nowhere.

"Our people attempted to contact you several times since Dr. Malvor made his request," Grayson said. "It proved to be impossible."

"Ah, yes." Ravinton shook his head. "The phone lines have been down all week. Bernard has been unable to determine the source of the problem, though we had a storm the other day that I suspect is responsible."

A storm knocked down the phone lines. Plausible. An enemy cutting the phone lines, on the other hand, was also possible and far too dangerous to discount, particularly when they only had his word to go on.

"Now," Ravinton said, "I understand that you are Thomas's friends?"

"We've been sent to escort him," Grayson explained.

"But you *are* his friends?"

"He and I met a long time ago," Rita said. "So in that sense, you could say we're friends."

"Oh?"

"We met during the war," she elaborated.

"And while I have never met him before," Grayson added, "you can rest assured I will do everything in my power to protect him."

"I see." The simple statement carried a note of disappointment, as if Ravinton had hoped for a different answer. Peculiar behavior.

Moreover, there was something off about his body language. Rita kept her face carefully neutral while she tried to observe him to see what was wrong. He seemed nervous, fidgeting slightly in his seat in a way out of sorts with the rest of his demeanor.

Neither he nor Bernard had made any effort to confirm their identities, either. Granted, that might be why he had attempted to clarify whether or not Malvor had met them before, but it still seemed odd. If they understood the danger, they ought to put more of an effort into confirming exactly who they had allowed into the mansion. The strange atmosphere of this place might be making her paranoid, but something about the situation simply felt wrong.

Ravinton abruptly rose, with no indication as to why.

The drawing room doors opened again, and Bernard returned with another man behind him who had to be Malvor, although he'd changed a lot over the past ten years. His hair had thinned out and his mannerisms weren't quite so owlish, although the white lab coat he wore seemed a size too large for him and flapped around him as he walked. If Simmons hadn't refreshed her memory about who he was, she'd likely have dismissed him as a complete stranger.

"Oh, praise the heavens!" He threw his hands into the air and walked into the drawing room. He looked at Ravinton. "Aleister, isn't it wonderful? We can finally stop worrying!"

"Indeed." Ravinton slowly sat down again.

At the same time, Grayson rose from his seat. "Dr. Thomas Malvor, I presume?"

"Yes, of course!"

"I am Edgar Grayson. Rita and I will be your escorts to Washington, where you will be placed under the government's official protection."

Rita stood up as well. "It's good to see you again after all this time, Dr. Malvor." Best not to mention that she wouldn't have recognized him.

"All this time?" He tilted his head, then blinked at her. "Why yes, aren't you the government agent who rescued me?"

"Hey, you finally got it right!" Now she *definitely* couldn't admit she didn't recognize him.

Malvor rubbed the back of his neck with a sheepish smile. "It's been so long, I almost didn't recognize you. What a coincidence to see you again like this."

"Not quite. I was assigned to come out here for you specifically because we have a history together."

"I'm so glad you two are here. Ever since this started, I've been worried sick about what would happen to me. My research is a wonderful thing, but I never imagined it would lead to people making attempts on my life! If Aleister hadn't offered me a place here, I don't know what would have happened to me."

Ravinton inclined his head in acknowledgment, although the motion seemed strained.

From the door, Bernard bowed. "Is there anything else you require, sir?"

"Nothing for me at this time," Ravinton looked at them. "Would you like anything? Refreshments?"

Rita shook her head, and Malvor waved his hand in a vague gesture that was probably meant to be dismissal, but Grayson cleared his throat. "A glass of water, if possible."

"A glass of water for Mr. Grayson," Ravinton said.

Bernard nodded and left the room.

While they waited, Grayson pulled out a small device, which he waved through the air to detect any sign of listening bugs. He shook his head. "No sign of any electronic interference. We should be safe to talk."

"Oh dear." Malvor stared at him with wide eyes. "You don't think those people who are after my life might try to eavesdrop on me here, do you?"

"It's possible," Rita said. Not to mention their host himself being on the list of suspects.

Yet Ravinton nodded with a grave expression. "You are free to check any part of the mansion."

"Do you have any reason to suspect you might be under surveillance?" Grayson asked.

The other man hesitated. "No… but while I like to think my mansion is secure, it is always better to take precautions. I would never forgive myself if my own inattention led to my friend's life being in danger."

Malvor ran a hand through his hair. "How did it come to this…? Is my research truly so important?"

"The government thinks so," Rita said, "and apparently our country's enemies will go to great lengths to prevent you from turning it over to us, so they must think so as well. You're a brilliant man, it seems."

He laughed weakly. "I would gladly exchange some brilliance to no longer be in this situation."

"Rest assured," Grayson said, "we will get you to safety as soon as possible. How soon can you be packed?"

Malvor's eyes widened. "What? Now?"

"It is imperative that we escort you back at once."

"But—"

The drawing room doors opened again, and Bernard returned with a glass of water. He held it out to Grayson. "Here you are, sir."

"Thank you." Grayson accepted it, looked it over and sniffed it as if checking for poison, then took two of his fake pills.

Malvor blinked. "Are you ill?"

"Everything will be fine as long as I take my medicine regularly," Grayson said. He handed the glass back to Bernard. "Thank you again. That is all I need."

"Very well, sir."

Their host stood up. "I shall retire to my study to give you time to catch up and discuss your plans. Simply ring for Bernard if you need to find me." He walked to the doors, nodded to Bernard, and the two of them walked to the door together.

"W-Wait!" Malvor jumped to his feet with a quaver in his voice. "You won't do anything that might disrupt my experiment, will you?"

Rita glanced between them. There was sudden tension in the air that hadn't been there a moment ago.

"I left in such a rush when I heard my escorts had arrived that I didn't properly put my equipment away yet. It's all quite sensitive, so any interruption or sudden movement could ruin all my hard work!"

"I have no intention of going near your equipment," Ravinton said smoothly. "I know how important your work is to you. As I said, I'm going to my study."

"Oh, good." Malvor rubbed the back on his neck with a laugh. "Sorry, I just get so nervous thinking that something might go wrong."

"I fully understand." Ravinton nodded again, and then he swept out of the room with Bernard right behind him.

Rita rubbed her chin. Everything else seemed on the level so far—at least on the surface. There was no sign that Malvor was being forced to stay here, or that anything would interfere with them taking him away.

But at the same time… something didn't feel quite right.

She waited a few seconds, then stood up and walked to the door. She listened, then opened it a crack. No sign of anyone out in the foyer. Since Grayson had already swept the room for bugs, they should be able to talk freely.

She returned to the couch. "As we said before, Dr. Malvor, our intention is to take you out of here as quickly as possible. Will that be a problem?"

The scientist fiddled with the edges of his sleeves. "Well… yes, it will."

Grayson frowned. "Why?"

"Because of my experiment! I can't leave until I've finished with my experiment!"

They exchanged glances.

"Aleister graciously allowed me to use his basement to work on my research. I have a new experiment in-progress as we speak, and I'm seeing fantastic results! But if I left now, all my work would have to be redone." He gave them a pleading look.

Great. The mad scientist was conducting experiments in the basement of the vampire's creepy mansion. This couldn't get any more ridiculous than it already was.

"Your life may be in danger the longer you stay here," Grayson said. "For your own safety, it is imperative that you leave at once."

"Aleister would never let anyone in here who might seek to do me harm!"

"And what if someone tricks him?" Rita asked. "He made no attempt to check our identities before allowing us in. Someone else could pretend to be a friend of yours and deceive him."

Malvor adjusted his glasses. "W-Well, I understand it might be dangerous, b-but you don't know how much completing this work means to me…"

"Is it worth your life?" Grayson asked.

"And what about your friend's life?" Rita shook her head. "Someone who comes here targeting you might hurt Count Ravinton and Bernard. It was kind of him to offer you a place to stay, but it's putting them in danger. The sooner you're out of here, the safer you'll be."

The scientist's shoulders slumped, and Rita held her breath in anticipation, but then he looked up at them with new hope shining in his eyes. "But the two of you are here now! You can protect Aleister and Bernard while I finish! Right? That's the sort of thing you're trained for, right?"

She sighed and looked at Grayson. "Maybe we should let him stay and finish his experiment after all. It's hardly an escort if we have to drag him out of here

"B-but you don't know how much completing this work means to *me*..."

by force." It was bad form to do that sort of thing. He was supposed to be going to the government by choice, not being abducted. "We should be able to guard him here well enough."

He pinched the bridge of his nose. "How much time do you need?"

"Just one more day."

"Meaning tomorrow night, we will be able to depart?"

"Yes, yes, of course!"

He sighed. "Fine."

Malvor's eyes lit up. "Thank you! Thank you so much. I'll never forget this for as long as I live; you've done a magnificent favor for both me and the field of science today!"

"Yes, yes," Grayson said, "but more importantly, we'll need to take extra precautions and stay alert for any threats."

"Speaking of which," Rita said, "how has Count Ravinton behaved since you arrived? Any peculiarities?"

"Wha—" Malvor stared at her with wide eyes. "Surely you don't suspect him!"

"I'm just trying to get a better understanding of the situation."

"Hmm…" He tilted his head from side to side, then spoke up. "Well, it's probably nothing, since he is my dear friend after all, but I suppose it *is* unusual… Every now and then, I've seen him sneaking around."

She raised her eyebrows. "Sneaking?"

"Yes, as if he didn't want to be seen." Uncertainty ran through Malvor's nervous laugh. "That's impossible, of course. He'd have no reason to sneak around in his own home. Besides, the only other people here are me and Bernard, and what could he possibly have to hide from us?"

Rita glanced at Grayson, and he met her gaze with a thoughtful expression. What indeed.

"By the way," she asked, "have you ever seen him in the sunlight?"

Malvor stared at her like she'd lost her mind. "What? I, err… yes? I think so. Why?"

She ignored the way Grayson's expression had rapidly changed from thoughtful to furious. "Just checking."

"If you repeat that asinine theory one more time, I might be forced to leave the premises immediately."

Rita folded her arms and met Grayson's glare. After agreeing to let Malvor stay one more day, they inspected the guest rooms provided to them by their host. Unfortunately, his sweep turned up listening devices in both rooms. He'd located the one in her room and taken it to his so he could study them both later, then returned so they could talk without being overheard.

And the moment she'd suggested discussing the situation, he'd immediately responded with that.

"I didn't even say anything yet," she said. "And besides, you'd never abandon a mission like that. That would be irresponsible and unprofessional."

He folded his arms with a scowl. "After you had the gall to make a mockery of this serious situation by asking Malvor such a question, you are in no position to question my work ethic."

"Look, I just thought we should get the sunlight question out of the way."

"It is utterly ridiculous!"

"You should keep an open mind." She grinned and leaned back against the wall. "I've seen some wild things on past missions. So go on, tell me. Why is it such a mockery that I asked about Ravinton going out in the sun?"

Grayson scowled. "Because vampires aren't restricted to coming out only at night. That was an invention of cinema."

Having expected his sentence to end with *don't exist*, Rita found herself thrown for a loop by his declaration. "Sorry, what?"

"Folklore about vampires never said a thing about them burning up in the sunlight or only walking around at night. Even the original *Dracula* never made any such claims; in fact, Dracula is seen to walk around during the daytime at multiple points in the book, though his power is much more muted compared to night. It was only in 1922's *Nosferatu* when they decided to introduce this new addition to a vampire's limitations, which since then has become quite popular. Therefore, it is wholly irrelevant to how an actual vampire, if such a creature existed, would behave. Unless you are suggesting that Ravinton is deliberately cultivating a vampire image whilst lacking knowledge of the original folklore, your question about the sunlight is both unnecessary and insulting!"

Rita stared at him. A slow grin spread across her face.

"What?" he snapped.

"So you're some sort of vampire purist?"

His scowl only deepened. "I have a working knowledge of literature and folklore, and I prefer to see it portrayed accurately."

She covered her mouth to hide her laughter. Here she thought he had no personality at all, but apparently there were a few topics besides work that caught his attention. He seemed to take her misunderstanding of vampires personally. Not only that, but it implied he would accept a vampire theory as plausible as long as it was grounded in accurate folklore.

He glowered. "What now?"

"Nothing." She shook her head. "Just glad that I got partnered with the vampire expert."

A flush crept up his neck, and he looked away. "So long as you understand."

It was tempting to needle him further, but she decided to have mercy for now. The mission came first, and they'd wasted too much time on this conversation already. "All right, so that leaves us with the most important matter of the hour: why were our rooms bugged?"

Grayson's glower deepened, but this time with good reason. "Things might not be as safe here as we presumed. Ravinton has made no move to oppose us, but we have yet to attempt to remove Malvor from the premises. He might have anticipated the scientist's refusal."

"You think he's our enemy after all?"

"We cannot rule out that possibility."

"If that's the case, then Dr. Malvor could be in immediate danger. If there's any chance that the threat to his life is already here in the mansion, then we need to find him at once and keep him under constant guard."

Rita walked down the mansion staircase and tried to look as though she belonged, even though she felt like an intruder. They had knocked on the door that belonged to Malvor, but it seemed he hadn't retired for the night yet. So while Grayson searched the mansion for any potential threats, Rita was tasked with finding out just where the elusive scientist had vanished to.

Downstairs, she barely had time to look around before she heard a man clear his throat behind her. She turned around.

Bernard bowed. "Is there anything I can help you with, ma'am?"

"Yes, actually. I wanted to talk to Dr. Malvor, but he isn't in his room."

"Then he is most likely in the basement. That is where he conducts his experiments, and he spends a great deal of time there."

Of course, the all-important experiments that meant he couldn't leave just yet. Rita rubbed her forehead. "Could you show me to the basement?"

"He is quite particular about not being disturbed during his work. If I might suggest an alternative, you could wait for him in the drawing room."

"I'm afraid that won't work."

"But—"

"I'll take full responsibility if he gets angry with me for interrupting."

Bernard sighed and nodded. "Very well, ma'am. Follow me."

He led her through the entrance hall and into a back corridor, while she tried to figure him out. He'd seemed reluctant to take her to the basement. Either Malvor was a terror when angry, or something else motivated him. He looked like a harmless old butler, but it wasn't inconceivable that he was their enemy. In fact, he would be in an ideal position to take advantage of Malvor's trust in Ravinton.

The corridor connected to a storage room, and Bernard opened a door at the back. Stairs led down into darkness, with a dim light at the top illuminating the steps enough to see. Distant noises came from down below, likely the experiment in progress.

"All right," she said. "Thanks."

Alert for any sign of trickery, she started down the stairs. Bernard kept the basement door open, which was a relief, although if he tried to lock them in, she was prepared to break out.

The stairs were narrow and musty, and the noises from the basement grew louder with each step she took. At last, her feet touched the solid cement floor, only for her to be confronted by another door right in front of her.

She tried the knob, but it was locked. She tried knocking. "Dr. Malvor?" Noises continued to come from the basement. She rapped harder to be heard over the sounds. "Dr. Malvor, I need to speak with you!"

"Just a minute!" Malvor shouted from the other side.

The noise grew louder still, and then the door opened.

He looked out of breath and frazzled, hair in disarray and a notebook held in one hand. He stepped back to let her into the basement room.

His setup looked as much like a mad scientist's laboratory as any she'd ever seen in movies. It certainly wasn't the neat, tidy arrangement of the labs back at HQ. Mysterious apparatuses covered the desks in the room, and lights blinked rapidly with no apparent cause. Everything hummed, so loud it felt like her teeth were rattling from standing this close. Bemused, Rita stared at it all for a moment. Nothing here told her why the government was so anxious to get his research data.

"Is something wrong?" Malvor asked.

"Sorry about this," she said. "I hope I didn't mess up your experiment."

"Oh, it's no trouble." He shook his head. "Um, did you need me for something?"

Well, that was a far milder reaction than she expected. "It occurred to us that if there are people after your life, they might attempt to breach the mansion and attack you here. We can't count on security staying intact with only a single employee working here. So one of us will stay with you at all times from now on for your protection."

Malvor waved his hands. "Oh, there's no need for that."

"It's better to be safe than sorry."

A basement in an old home like this could contain its share of secrets, too. She did a quick sweep of the room with her scanner. Malvor's equipment threw off a ton of electromagnetic interference that made it impossible to determine if the room was bugged or not. She frowned. Come to think of it, she knew very little about the nature of the Malvor Report beyond it being related to radar and missile guidance.

"I appreciate your concern," Malvor said. "Really! You two are going to so much trouble to protect me. But I really do need to finish up this experiment before we go..."

"I didn't mean you had to leave," Rita said. "I'll just wait nearby, and I promise I won't touch anything." She grinned and winked. "Don't worry, my presence alone doesn't cause machinery to explode."

He didn't appear amused by her attempt at humor. "This experiment is quite sensitive and classified... or at least it will be once I officially make a deal with the government."

"I don't understand a thing I'm seeing anyway."

"Even so, I..." His shoulders slumped. "I hate to ask something like this of the person trying to save my life, but do you have the required security clearances to see the details of my research?"

Rita furrowed her brow. "Well, no." No one had said anything about that.

"Then... I'm sorry, but perhaps you could wait outside this room instead?"

She sighed and surveyed the basement. There weren't any other visible exits, not even a tiny window. "All right. As long as I stay near the door, there shouldn't be any trouble. If anything happens, shout for me, all right?"

"Yes, yes, of course. Thank you so much!"

She turned back toward the door, and the whir of electricity intensified behind her. As she stepped left, she glanced back over her shoulder. Malvor scribbled frantic notes and occasionally adjusted a dial on his machine. His concern about security clearances was a reasonable one, and yet...

She closed the door and walked up the basement stairs.

Bernard was still waiting for her in the storage room. He bowed when he saw her. "Is everything all right, ma'am?"

"Yes, but could you tell my partner, Mr. Grayson, to join me in the base ment?"

"Certainly!" The butler bowed again and left.

Well, he was certainly accommodating. Rita looked around the storage room and examined the basement stairs while she waited. Nothing about this room looked suspicious.

At last, the door opened again, and Grayson walked in. "What's the situation?"

"Malvor is down in the basement conducting experiments."

"Why aren't you in there with him?"

"He wouldn't let me stay for security reasons."

Grayson made a discontented sound but said nothing.

"How did your investigation go?" she asked.

"No sign of any threats," he said. "However, I located several more bugs throughout the mansion."

She winced. "Great. So the mansion is definitely under surveillance. Did Ravinton say anything?"

"When I began, I requested a copy of the mansion blueprints, which he relinquished without complaint. I saw him watching me as I searched, but he kept his distance."

Interesting. "What are you going to do?"

"I attempted to trace the signal from the bugs, but some sort of interference is getting in the way."

"That would be Malvor's experiment. The electronic interference in the basement is ridiculous."

Grayson's grim expression darkened further. "I'll work on a plan for security. Then I'll see if I can learn anything from these bugs; if not, I'll destroy them."

"Got it. I'll guard Malvor in the meantime."

He left, and Rita descended the stairs once more to station herself outside the basement room door.

Everything made sense. Security clearances were a valid concern. Any scientist would be wary of an outsider seeing their work. Electronic interference was perfectly harmless, too. Yet, when she considered everything that had happened since they arrived at the mansion, something about this didn't feel right.

Twenty minutes later, Malvor emerged from the basement. "Excellent progress! Now I'm ready to sleep!" He started up the stairs at a jaunty pace.

Rita followed. "Are you still on track to leave tomorrow evening?"

"Oh yes, without a doubt! I'll pack up the pieces of equipment I need to take with me, while Aleister can dispose of the rest."

At least they didn't have any further complications there. They reached the first floor, then continued up together to the second floor, where Grayson paced in the hallway outside the guest rooms. He turned to face them when they arrived.

"Any progress?" Rita inquired.

"I've kept a handful of the bugs for further analysis and destroyed the others I found."

Malvor blinked. "You mean there were more listening devices?"

"Quite a few."

"Oh dear..."

Grayson folded his arms. "While I'm certain you value your privacy, I think it would be for the best if we share a room tonight in case anything happens, as I have been unable to ascertain how your enemies gained access to the mansion in the first place."

"All right then." Malvor laughed. "It will be a refreshing change to have company!"

That was a relief. Given his stubbornness about other matters, Rita had expected him to object or insist there wasn't that much danger. Maybe the reality of his situation finally sank in.

Grayson handed Rita a bundle of thick papers that appeared to be the blueprints he'd mentioned. "Here. I've marked the locations of any potential weak points and vulnerabilities—doors, windows, and so on. Memorize them in case of emergency."

"You got it."

He frowned.

"What?" she asked.

"You're actually taking this seriously."

"Wait, did you really think I wouldn't?"

He just shook his head, though the faintest of smiles crossed his face. With a nod to Malvor, he beckoned the scientist down the hall to the guest room he'd been given.

Rita retired into her own guest room and unfolded the blueprints. Grayson had done a thorough job. Every spot was marked not only with a note about what type of vulnerability it was, but also with theories about how an assault from that spot would be conducted either alone or in concert with other attacks.

She scanned the blueprints to memorize the most likely vulnerabilities on the first floor and second floor, then flipped to the final page. She paused. This page showed the basement, one large room with an adjacent smaller room.

But she hadn't seen any sign of a second room down there.

A secret room and Malvor's insistence that she leave the basement during his experiment... She rubbed her chin and frowned at the blueprints. All the oddities since their arrival ran through her thoughts. It could be a coincidence, but a nagging suspicion in the back of her mind told her she'd regret leaving it at this.

She wondered what Grayson and Malvor were doing. They didn't seem to have anything in common. Perhaps Grayson was taking fake medicine and lecturing him on folklore. As for Ravinton and Bernard, they might keep late hours. It would be best to wait longer before attempting anything.

Because one thing had become clear. She needed to return to the basement.

Rita waited until midnight and then slipped out of her room and tiptoed down the hall. Even if everyone was asleep, she didn't want to take any chances. Whoever had bugged the mansion might still be listening.

Silence blanketed the manor as she crept down the stairs and headed toward the hallway Bernard had led her down to reach the basement. She pushed open the hallway door.

Quiet voices came from a room down the hall despite the late hour. She paused to listen.

One was Bernard. After a moment, she recognized the other voice as Ravinton.

"We should act now, while he's asleep."

"It's too dangerous, sir. You know what will happen if we're discovered. Even talking like this is a risk."

"Even so, persisting like this will get us nowhere!"

"An opportunity may present itself tomorrow, sir."

"Tomorrow might be too late!"

Rita pulled back from the doorway. Suspicious, but not enough to draw any conclusions from. It wouldn't be wise to linger here and be caught. She needed to find out what was going on in the basement before she could make any determinations. Careful to not let her footsteps give her away, she tiptoed past the occupied room and continued down the hall.

She crept into the storage room and opened the basement door. This time, she closed it behind herself to reduce the chances of discovery. Hand half-raised toward the light switch to turn it on, she hesitated, then got out her flashlight instead. Best to use as little light as possible.

With her flashlight lighting each step before her, she descended into the basement and reached the second door.

Locked.

She removed one of the lockpicks from her hairpiece and went to work on the door. This had never been her area of expertise, but she'd picked up some skills over the years. At last, the pins clicked into place and the doorknob turned. She twisted it and stepped into the dark basement room.

The equipment remained incomprehensible. She approached it and studied it more carefully under the flashlight's beam. While not a scientist, Rita had some familiarity with machines. It frustrated her to see a device that made no sense to her at all.

She walked from one end of the apparatus to the other and examined the entire machine. Then she frowned. Despite the general inscrutable nature of the machinery, the boxy part at the end was quite familiar indeed—it was a large radio concealed within an outer metal casing.

Perplexed, she decided to set aside the matter of the machine for now. The discrepancy with the basement blueprints needed to be investigated.

Using the stairs' location to figure out the orientation of the room, she looked at the wall where the door to the smaller adjoining room should be according to the blueprints. A bookshelf blocked that entire section of the wall, filled with scientific books. A recent addition from Malvor, perhaps?

She took a breath, then grabbed the edge of the bookshelf and pushed.

It slid much more easily than expected to reveal the missing door. Perhaps the bookshelf had been placed there intentionally for that purpose. The suspicions that took root in her mind earlier that evening flared. Malvor tried to keep her out of this basement, and he'd potentially hidden the door leading to the adjacent room.

The door was locked. Locked, hidden, and within a larger room that had itself been locked… her sense that the second basement room held something significant strengthened by the minute. She readied her lockpick again.

This lock was trickier, but finally gave way. She took a breath and pulled the door open.

Basic furniture including a bed and chair gave the second room a cozier appearance than the outer basement—or at least it would have if not for the most important detail. A man sat on the bed, manacled to the wall.

Rita rushed into the room. "Are you all right?"

The prisoner lifted his head, and she froze.

Ten years later, he still reminded her of an owl with how he blinked up at her in the dark room. Time had not changed him that much, not enough to make him unrecognizable. He looked worse for wear, though hope filled his eyes when he saw her.

"Dr. Malvor?" she asked, hardly able to believe it herself.

"You…" He blinked at her. "You're the WAC who saved me during the war!"

She might have laughed if the situation wasn't so dire. Malvor never remembered her role correctly, and she hadn't forgotten what he looked like.

The man upstairs calling himself Dr. Thomas Malvor was an imposter.

She hurried to his side and went to work on the manacles with her lockpicks. "What's going on here?" she asked. "Who's that guy pretending to be you?"

"You… you're the WAC who saved me during the war!"

Malvor shuddered. “I don’t know his name. He took me prisoner to force me to give him information about my research.”

“Is Aleister Ravinton in on it?”

“No—the man said he would kill me if Aleister or his butler revealed the truth.”

Rita nodded slowly. That explained why the entire mansion had been bugged. The imposter must have monitored Ravinton and Bernard whenever he wasn’t with them. Come to think of it, there were times when Ravinton acted strangely around her and Grayson, as well as the conversation she overheard between him and Bernard. They must be trying to figure out how to reveal the truth without endangering Malvor.

She undid the first manacle and started on the second. “What’s with the experiment he’s conducting in the basement? Is he trying to replicate your work?”

“I… I don’t think so. He always starts up that machine first, then comes in here to interrogate me. Once he’s done with me, he turns the machine off.”

If the so-called experiments had nothing to do with Malvor’s research after all, then that meant…

The radio. All the pieces fell into place. That was the true nature of the machine. It was simply a radio with extra pieces and blinking lights attached to the outer casing. The fake Malvor was transmitting anything he learned from his captive, with the radio disguised in order to avoid drawing suspicion from the agents on their way to meet with him. The electronic interference was probably intentional, too.

The second manacle came undone, and Malvor rubbed his wrists with a grateful smile.

“Have you told him anything?”

He hung his head. “Yes. I… I’ve never been strong. I don’t know how to resist when someone hurts me.”

She touched his shoulder. “It’s fine. I understand. The most important thing is getting you out of here alive. Can you walk?”

“I think so.”

Beckoning for him to follow, Rita left the secret room. Malvor followed at a much slower pace. He seemed to be in pain, but not enough to require help. That would make things at least mildly easier.

A terrible thought struck her. “Do you know if the imposter is monitoring this room?” Due to that interference, she hadn’t been able to check for bugs.

“I… I have wondered… if he was monitoring this room somehow…” Malvor looked down at the floor. “I mean… if he wasn’t… then Aleister would have come for me…”

Great. That made perfect sense. Ravinton would have known about the second room and realized where the hostage was being kept. Anytime the imposter was out of the basement, he or Bernard could have gone down there; even if they couldn't pick the lock, they could at least stop the imposter from getting to Malvor. The fact that they never tried meant they deemed it too dangerous.

She'd need to prepare for the worst-case scenario. Maybe rooming with Grayson meant the imposter couldn't monitor his listening devices, but she couldn't count on that. She had to act under the assumption that he already knew she'd found Malvor.

Would he storm in here? No, he wouldn't risk a direct confrontation without leverage. More likely he'd take Ravinton and Bernard hostage. He'd also need to take out Grayson.

But this imposter had no idea who he was dealing with.

Rita ran to the apparatus used for the phony experiments. Now that she knew it was just a radio with doodads and gizmos attached to it to make it look like a fancier piece of equipment, she was in her element.

Examining it from this perspective, it was a simpler setup than she had imagined. The imposter had two signals set up. One was simply audio monitoring of the basement so that if anyone breached it and found Malvor, he would be alerted. Likely he had the receiver somewhere on his person, perhaps a concealed earpiece.

The second was an external signal keyed to a specific location. This must be where he was transmitting information to whoever had sent him to get Malvor's research data. She made a few quick notes to turn in along with her report. If the Hand could use this information to deduce the location of the other party in the deal, that would go a long way toward tracking them down.

Then she changed it to the frequency of Grayson's wristwatch radio and took a moment to think of the right things to say.

Malvor watched her with a bewildered expression. "What are you doing?"

"Trying to contact my partner, but he's not answering." She spoke at a normal volume to be sure the radio picked it up, while attempting to sound casual enough to fool any eavesdroppers. "The imposter might have already made a move."

"What?!"

"He's far more deranged than I expected. I regret not anticipating this."

Step one, complete.

"We need to get you out of here as soon as possible." She stood up slowly, but made sure to leave the radio channel open. "I'll go out first. When I give the signal, follow me."

"All right."

Rita opened the door and cautiously climbed up the stairs. The storage room was clear. So was the hallway. She tiptoed down it, peering into each room as she went, until movement caught at the other end of the hall caught her eye.

Someone was coming. She slipped into the nearest room and held her breath, door open a crack so she could watch the hall.

The imposter entered the hallway with a gun in his hand. He headed straight for the room where Ravinton and Bernard had been talking earlier. Her heart sank. If she'd arrived just a little earlier, she might have been able to help them.

Alarmed voices cried out from inside.

"Shut up," the imposter ordered, his voice cold. "Keep your hands up and don't make any sudden moves."

"What are you going to do?" Ravinton's voice asked in response.

"One of our guests is about to come this way. You two will ensure her good behavior."

Rita nodded to herself. The fake Malvor was likely standing so that he could watch the door while keeping them covered. Notably, he didn't seem concerned about Grayson at all. Since he had just arrived and she hadn't heard any gunshots, that boded well for her plan.

She returned to the hall and retreated toward the storage room.

This situation was bad, but not unsalvageable. Grayson's whereabouts were unknown, but if he'd understood her message correctly, he should have been able to trick the imposter into thinking he was no longer a threat. Now she just had to get through this without bringing any harm to Malvor or the hostages.

The safest place for Malvor at the moment was the basement, ironically enough. And the best way to save the hostages was to disarm the imposter. Unfortunately, he was watching the hall. While the Hand issued some wonderful pieces of equipment to their agents, they had yet to develop one that could let her walk around unseen. She'd have to mention that to the boys at the lab. Invisibility would be a godsend in a situation like this.

But with no such fantasy coming to life, she'd have to work with what she had.

As quietly as possible, Rita returned to the basement. She opened the door, and Malvor fixed her with a wide-eyed stare. "What's wrong?" he asked. "I thought you were going to give me a signal."

"We've got a problem. The imposter has your friends held hostage."

"What?!"

"He's waiting for us to go past him, which means we need to find a solution that doesn't involve doing that."

"How? If he has Aleister and Bernard held captive, doesn't that mean he has the upper hand?"

"If we play into his hands, yes. However, we have an advantage. As long as we don't pass through the hallway like he expects, he can't issue any demands. That means the hostages are safe for now. All we have to do is not enter that hallway."

Malvor furrowed his brow. "Err… perhaps I'm misunderstanding something, but are you suggesting we spend the rest of our lives in this basement? I suppose it's warm enough, but there is a decided lack of food."

She pinched the bridge of her nose. "Of course I'm not suggesting we live here."

"Oh. Then what *is* your plan?"

She winked. "You forget, I managed to find you in the first place. Those blueprints are a lot more revealing than the imposter likely realizes. I'll have you out of here in no time, and then we can save the hostages."

The implication, of course, was that she knew of a second way to the leave the basement. If the imposter was still eavesdropping, he'd have no choice but to act.

Either oblivious or playing his part well, Malvor fiddled with his sleeves nervously. "What do you want me to do?"

She rubbed her chin. Tempting though it was to take him up the stairs and hide him in one of the other rooms along the way to the basement, so that when the imposter came for her, he'd be safely out of the way, there was an off chance the imposter would check the rooms instead of heading straight to the basement. Then he'd be in more danger than ever.

Instead, she pointed to the adjacent room where he'd been locked up. "Go in there."

"In there? But that's—"

"Trust me."

Malvor stared at her for a moment, then slowly walked back toward the secret room. When he reached the entrance, he paused and looked back at her. "You… do know what you're doing, don't you?"

"Who do you think you're talking to?" She winked. "That imposter doesn't know who he's messing with. I've got this. Before you know it, we'll be on our way out of here."

Although some of her confidence was feigned, it did the trick. He shot her a relieved smile before heading into the secret room. Rita closed the door behind him. With any luck, the imposter wouldn't be certain enough of Malvor's location to do anything rash.

The basement door opened.

Rita drew her gun and aimed it at the door. The imposter stepped onto the stairs with Bernard in front of him, held at gunpoint. "Drop the gun, or the old man gets it."

She dropped her gun with a sigh. It had been worth a try. "You sure you should be calling other people old?" He had the years to make his guise as Malvor believable, after all.

The man snorted and said nothing as he forced Bernard down into the basement. The old butler was shaking, eyes wide, clearly terrified. He had his hands held in the air and took each step cautiously, as if afraid a wrong move might lead to his death.

As expected, the imposter hadn't attempted to bring both hostages down here. Presumably Ravinton was tied up; he wouldn't risk losing his greater leverage over Malvor by killing him. Grayson's whereabouts were still unknown. If he was alive—she shuddered; for all their arguments, she hoped he was alive and had understood her signal correctly—he might find Ravinton and free him, which would shift the odds in their favor.

He was annoying, he was stuffy, he was a pain—and if anyone could pick up on what she meant with her cryptic radio message and respond to it, it was him. He would likely be preparing for her next signal at this moment. As much as it pained her to admit it, he was a good partner for a mission like this.

And that meant she had to stall for time.

"Interesting setup you've got here," Rita said with a nod toward the equipment. "If you aren't the real Dr. Malvor, what exactly were you trying to do with all of this, imitate his experiment?"

"Don't play coy," the imposter said sharply. "You know perfectly well it's a radio transmitter."

"Do I?"

"I know your history with the Hand. Some call you Radio Rita. You'd recognize its true purpose in an instant if you were left alone to investigate it."

"Maybe I headed straight for the hidden room instead," she said. "So thanks for telling me it's a radio transmitter. That answers a lot of questions."

"This charade is pointless. Anything you think you learned won't mean a thing once you're dead."

She sighed. "You know, I liked you better when you were pretending to be a meek little scientist."

"And I liked you better when you believed that's all I was."

"Exactly what did you intend to do, have us escort you to Washington?"

"Indeed. We would have left here together and all would have been well."

"And the real Malvor?"

"I'd have killed him, of course."

"You're a heartless man, Mr…" She raised her eyebrows. "What should I call you now, anyway? Obviously your real name isn't Thomas Malvor."

"A dead woman has no need for my name."

"If you simply intended to kill me, you'd have come down here blasting instead of bringing a hostage and engaging me in conversation. You must want something from me. What is it?"

The imposter raised his eyebrows. "First, you're going to tell me everything you know."

"Sorry, but I don't know anything."

"That is highly unlikely for someone in your position."

So he wanted information about the Hand. She narrowed her eyes and studied him. Everything suggested he came into this situation expecting to be countered by their agents. He wasn't just someone who wanted Malvor's research, then, but someone willing to oppose the government directly. In that case, he was even more dangerous.

"Will you tell me?" he repeated.

"I have no intention of saying anything to you."

"Even if it puts this poor man's life in danger?"

Bernard's eyes widened in panic.

Despite a pang of sympathy, Rita kept her voice steady. "You just admitted to me your original plan was to kill Dr. Malvor after getting all his information. I have every reason to believe you'll kill your hostage even if I *do* talk. Now, if you put down that gun and let the poor man leave, I might reconsider."

With a sigh, the imposter snapped his fingers.

Two men burst into the basement and ran down the stairs.

Oh. So it wasn't a solo operation after all. They must have been hiding outside the mansion until the imposter realized something had gone wrong and had them join him to await a signal. Rita sighed and reassessed the situation. As long as Malvor didn't panic and put himself in danger trying to help, it should still be possible to get out of this. With Bernard at gunpoint, she couldn't fight back just yet, so she settled for pressing the edge of her bracelet against her leg.

The two men closed in and grabbed her, one on each side. They tightened their grips on her arms as if to emphasize her current helpless position.

"Let's start over," the imposter said. "You're going to tell me everything you know."

The sound of tolling church bells rang out from Rita's bracelet. Everyone jolted in surprise, and she took advantage to break free of her captors. She made a break for the door.

"One more step and I shoot him!" The imposter jammed his gun into the back of Bernard's neck, and the old man cried out in fear.

Rita froze. She lifted her hands into the air.

The two men caught her again and dragged her back into position in front of the imposter. One of them ripped her bracelet free and tossed it to him.

He eyed it. "Interesting. I don't know what you hoped to achieve with that little stunt, but we'll find out in due time."

"This isn't very gentlemanly of you," Rita said. "If you're going to interrogate me, must we do it in the basement? A five-star hotel would do wonders for my mood."

"You are in no position to make jokes."

"So you claim."

"Surely you have realized by now that I have a great deal of practice with this sort of thing. Getting information from you will be no challenge." He shook his head slowly. "You are a lovely woman. It would be a pity to have to damage you."

"Now that was almost a compliment. You're getting better, but still not good enough to make me want to talk."

"By the time we're finished with you, you'll tell us everything we want to know."

"Hah! I've never cracked! Well, there was this one time with a truth serum, but you strike me as more of the 'torture' sort."

"It is quite effective at loosening tongues that are otherwise still."

"Now there's one thing I've never been accused of." Rita smirked.

"Your show of bravado will get you nowhere." He snapped his fingers. "Tie—"

The basement door flew open. The imposter turned, but not in time to stop Grayson as he charged down the stairs and tackled him away from Bernard. With the hostage no longer in immediate danger, Rita fought back against her captors. She kicked one and twisted free.

She crossed the floor to the terrified Bernard and shoved him toward the door to the second room. "Hide in there!"

"What?!"

"Go!"

With him taken care of, Rita turned in time to counter one of the men running at her. She elbowed him in the stomach and knocked him away from her. Then she glanced toward the stairs.

Grayson's large build was working to his advantage. He grabbed the imposter by the shoulders and simply threw him across the room.

Well, that was one away to do it.

The second man ran at her, so Rita had no further time to dwell on Grayson's straightforward combat style. She ducked under her attacker's swing and kicked him. The other one circled around to try to sneak up on her from behind, but she moved just as he lunged forward. She grabbed his arm and used his momentum to fling him over her shoulder. He hit the floor with a groan, and she spun around to face the other one again. Two against one made this difficult without a weapon to even the odds.

"A little help would be nice!" she shouted to Grayson.

The imposter made a break for the door only to find Grayson in his path. Grayson stayed focused on him. "I thought you could handle anything!"

"Wait, you're not seriously letting me fight them by myself just to make a point, are you?" She tackled her assailant by the legs to knock him to the floor, but the other opponent made it to his feet and grabbed her shoulders. "This is becoming a brawl!"

"It's your own fault for not having a weapon with you."

"I didn't expect things to fall apart this quickly!"

Grayson pinned the imposter against the wall and raised his voice loud enough to be heard over the sounds of their struggle. "I have your leader! Let her go now if you want him to remain unharmed!"

The second attacker wrapped his hands around Rita's neck, and she kicked out behind her. It broke his grip, but that meant she lost her hold on the other man, who threw her against the floor.

"I don't think they care!" she shouted.

Grayson sighed and punched the imposter in the jaw. He slumped to the floor, unconscious. Without further delay, Grayson charged toward them. Rita rolled out of the way and scrambled to her feet. With him helping at last, it took only a couple of minutes to subdue the other two.

She caught her breath and dusted herself off. "Thanks for the help."

He furrowed his brow with a deep frown.

"What?" she asked.

"I didn't know you were capable of sincere gratitude."

"Just when I start to like you, you say something snide."

"Excuse me? You're starting to like me?"

"Don't let it go to your head. I'm already reconsidering."

He shook his head. "Anyway, where is the real Dr. Malvor?"

"Oh, right." Rita raised her voice. "Dr. Malvor! Bernard! It's safe to come out now!"

The door leading to the other room opened, and both men emerged. Despite having avoided the actual fight, they looked as harried as if they'd been throwing punches themselves.

"Are you all right?" Malvor asked. "It sounded dangerous!"

"Don't worry." Rita waved her hand in a dismissive gesture. "They never stood a chance against us."

Grayson snorted. "All the same, let's get them out of here before they wake up."

"And reassure poor Aleister!" Malvor said.

"I saw him on my way down here," Grayson said. "He's shaken, but unharmed."

"Oh, thank goodness."

"Then we can finally get you out of here, Dr. Malvor." Rita paused. "Unless you're going to say you have some experiments to finish up first."

"Oh, no." Malvor shook his head with wide eyes. "I would never do something like that."

"*Good.*"

Simmons set the report aside and looked up at them. "Well, Dr. Malvor has turned over his research to our scientists and will remain in protective custody until we can be certain the threat to him has passed. Everything is proceeding according to schedule. Even better, the information you obtained from the radio has helped us to track down the people the imposter was working for."

"Glad to hear it," Rita said.

She and Grayson stood together in front of Simmons's desk. After bringing Malvor safely to headquarters and turning over the imposter and his cohorts, they had submitted a full report about what happened.

"The imposter's contacts don't appear to have been connected to any specific government," Simmons said, "so we're still attempting to determine their identities."

"What?" Rita frowned. "That guy was expecting us. He knew who we worked for. That doesn't exactly sound like your regular old rogue corporation."

He nodded with a grave frown. "Depending on what we learn, we might need to call on the two of you to investigate this matter further."

"I will do everything to the best of my ability," Grayson said.

"Wait," Rita said, "when you say 'the two of us,' you don't mean Grayson and I working together again, do you?"

Grayson's eyes widened.

"Why not?" Simmons raised his eyebrows. "You performed admirably on this mission."

"This was a one-time deal," she argued. "You know I work better with Misha than anyone else!"

Grayson nodded. "With all due respect, sir, I think it is most efficient to partner her with someone able to get along with her."

"What's that supposed to mean?" she asked. "You're the one who's hard to get along with, not me."

"I beg to differ."

"Of course you do."

"I'll keep your requests under consideration," Simmons said, in the tone of one who fully intended to make them work together again someday, perhaps even for his own amusement. "In the meantime, you should both get some rest. After what you accomplished, you deserve it."

"Anyone would need rest after dealing with her," Grayson said under his breath.

Rita raised her eyebrows. "Which of us got pedantic over vampire folklore again?"

"Paying close attention to details doesn't mean I was being pedantic."

"Yes it does."

"Just because you refuse to take these things seriously—"

"Are you actually chiding me for not taking *vampires* seriously enough?"

Still bickering, they left the office and continued down the hall. Despite everything, Rita smiled. All right, she could deal with this if she had to. If the two of them had to work together again someday, it wouldn't be the end of the world. He might have no personality, but he pulled through for her when it counted.

Misha came down the hallway in the opposite direction and smiled. "Rita, I heard you were back. Nothing exploded?"

"That was one time," she said.

"Don't change the tally now."

Grayson furrowed his brow. "Are you telling me this woman has been trusted with explosives?"

"*Trusted* is stretching the definition of the word."

Rita folded her arms. "Oh sure, I get back from a difficult mission and the first thing you do is start slandering me."

"It's not slander when it's true."

"I think I should hear this story," Grayson said.

"Fine," Rita said, "but then I'm going to be present for it. Drinks are on me."

Maybe all three of them would end up working together someday. Somehow, that didn't sound as terrible as she once would have imagined. With the possibility that the imposter worked for a dangerous organization, it was good to have more people she could count on.

For now, they would rest, relax, and prepare for the net mission. Whatever the future held, it certainly wouldn't be boring.

THE END

Radio Rita and the Impossible Story

Here we are at the end of "Radio Rita and the Malvor Report," and what a long, strange journey it was to reach this point.

When I learned there were plans for a second Radio Rita collection, I signed up right away. I'd wanted to write another story featuring my incarnation of the character, and while I didn't have anything specific planned, it didn't take too long to pull together some ideas. I figured I'd have it done in a couple of months.

Instead, it took an entire year.

My initial idea for the sequel involved Rita and Misha being assigned to escort a female scientist. She had a body double who would be assigned to Rita, with her goal being to draw public attention while Misha escorted the actual scientist to her destination. The twist was that the body double was actually the real scientist only pretending to be her body double, *and* she was also the story's villain. An early scene would have her visit the radio station and use it to secretly send her own coded message to the other villains. However, this version of the story never went very far. Every time I sat down to write it, I had no motivation. I worked on some variations, such as Rita and the scientist ending up on an island where she'd begin nefarious experiments, but I finally decided to give up and start fresh.

The second incarnation of the sequel involved Rita and Misha escorting a scientist named Grayson to an isolated mansion, where he was to meet with the reclusive Dr. Malvor to get his research data. Other people had also come to the mansion, including a scientist named Mason and his wife Gloria, who was the secretly-evil scientist from the first version of the story. In classic murder mystery style, a storm would strand them all at the mansion together, after which Malvor would turn up dead. I got significantly further in this version of the story, about halfway through before I realized I was just going through the motions—creating a hollow story that lacked soul because I had no true feeling for it.

Back to the drawing board! After looking at what worked in the second version, I realized Misha was getting in the way. He had no real role in the story; he was just there because he worked with Rita. So for the third attempt, I reworked Grayson the scientist into Grayson the agent who would be Rita's partner for the mission. They would escort Dr. Gloria Mason to meet with Dr. Malvor and get his research data at a formal ball. This version lasted two pages before I scrapped it.

Version four! Rita and Grayson would escort Mason to meet Malvor for his research data on an island, but not before Mason took advantage of the radio station to send out a coded message to the other villains. I made it all the way up to the radio scene and then lost motivation.

By this point, the story was beginning to feel impossible. Half a year had passed since I started. Every time I sat down to write, I wanted to work on other projects instead.

Something about the core of the story clearly wasn't working for me, and I realized I needed to abandon my attachment to the initial idea.

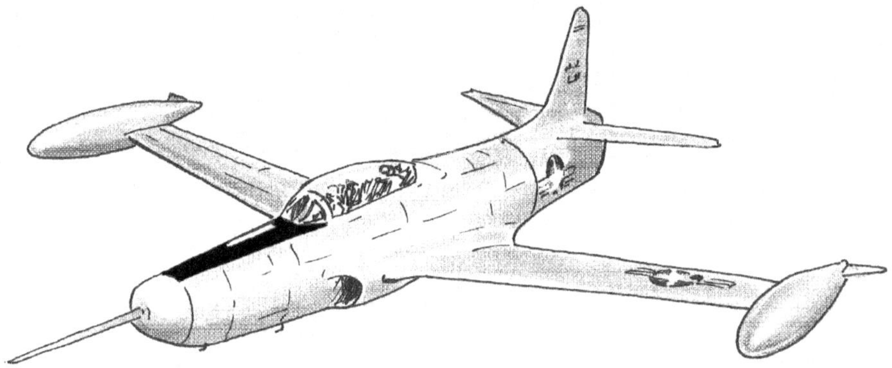

The Lockheed F-94 Starfire is a first-generation jet powered all-weather day/night interceptor aircraft designed and produced by Lockheed Corporation. It was the first operational United States Air Force (USAF) fighter equipped with an afterburner as well as being the first jet-powered all-weather fighter to enter combat during the Korean War.

In my fifth attempt, I got rid of Mason. She had been the main antagonist for every draft so far, but I had to try it without her. This new version saw Rita and Grayson heading out to get Malvor's research data from the isolated mansion where he had taken refuge with Count Ravinton, who was widely rumored to be a vampire. Thick treetops shrouded the mansion in total darkness, and someone—whom I eventually determined would be an imposter posing as Malvor—used tricks to confuse their sense of time and make them believe the vampire rumors were true. I wrote this draft through to the end.

At last, I had a version that was working! However, the vampire aspect felt a bit out of place and wasn't necessary for the plot, so I reduced it to a joke instead of widespread rumors. My only regret was losing one of my favorite lines: *"The man afraid of European accents is taking refuge with a vampire," Rita said. "You couldn't make this stuff up."*

With those changes in mind, I wrote the sixth and final version. Beta readers helped me fix up a few aspects, and then it was finally done. It felt entirely different from the story idea I originally started with… but looking back over all those attempts made me see how each one helped. Every failed draft contributed something that ended up in the final version.

It took me a whole year to reach the end of "Radio Rita and the Malvor Report," but I'm happy with how it turned out. Here's hoping you enjoyed it as well!

SAMANTHA LIENHARD - has been writing for most of her life, especially in the fantasy and horror genres. She graduated from Mansfield University with a B.A. in English and a minor in Creative Writing, and then from Seton Hill University with an M.F.A. in Writing Popular Fiction. When she isn't writing, she can usually be found playing video games. Her publications include a comedy novella called *The Zombie Mishap*, a Lovecraftian horror novella called *The Book at Dernier*, a Lovecraftian horror novelette called *It Came Back*, the pulp fiction story "The Domino Lady Takes the Case," and several short horror stories. She also writes for video games and has worked on the scripts for several indie titles, including *Ascendant Hearts*, *The Trials of Olympus III, Two Till Midnight,* and *Eternal Radiance.*

Information about all of her work can be found at her website: http://www.samanthalienhard.com

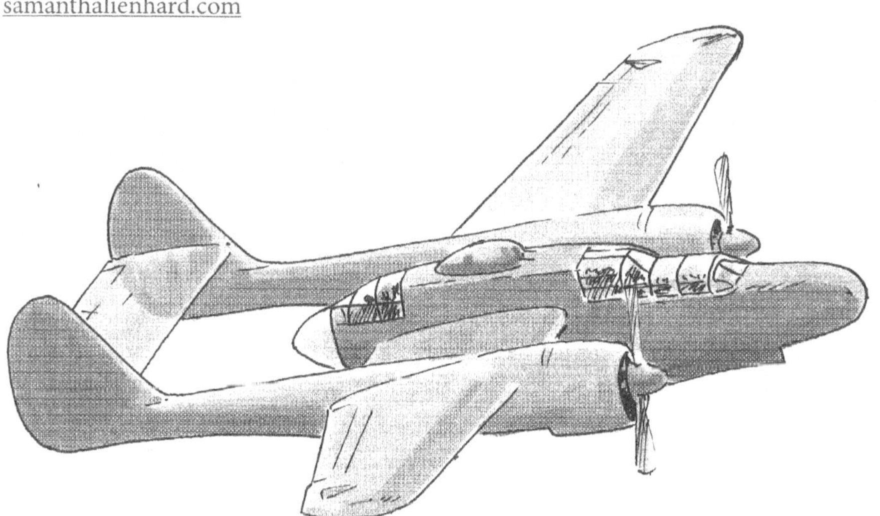

The Northrop P-61 Black Widow is a twin-engine United States Army Air Forces fighter aircraft of World War II. It was the first U.S. aircraft conceived from the outset and deployed operationally specifically as a night fighter, incorporating onboard radar as part of the original airframe design.

INTERIOR ILLUSTRATOR -

ROB DAVIS - is an award-winning artist with a 38-plus-year comic book and illustration career. With comics from Marvel, DC, Malibu, Innovation, Caliber and others Rob has worked on series depicting the crews of *Star Trek*'s original series, *the Next Generation*, and *Deep Space Nine*, and other TV series such as *Quantum Leap* and *Pirates of Dark Water.* Characters like Merlin, Robin Hood, Zorro, and Sherlock Holmes have all been subjects of Rob's work. He is presently the Art Director, Designer, and Illustrator for Pulp Revival publisher Airship 27 Productions. He also self-publishes some of his most recent comic book work via his Redbud Studio imprint and is a contributor to Silverline Comics. He is retired from "real work" and lives in central Missouri with his wife, two children, and grandchildren.

COVER ILLUSTRATOR-

MICHAEL YOUNGBLOOD —Of Asheville N.C. has a bachelor's degree in art and has done most of his work in architectural illustration and design. He's also done various other freelance projects since 1991.

The award-winning start of it all:

Airship 27 Productions is thrilled to announce the debut of pulpdom's newest hero, aviator Radio Rita. Envisioned originally as a pin-up representation of the publishing house by Managing Editor, Ron Fortier, the character took on a life of her own when several New Pulp writers suggested writing stories of the tall, action-loving redhead. Enticed by the idea, Fortier challenged writers to imagine their versions of the character from a set of four basic physical attributes. The result is four unique women, all of them Radio Rita. Buckle up for adventure, pulp fans. She's still one of a kind.

Volume one features tales by Teel James Glenn, Samantha Lienhard, Gene Moyers, and Mel Odom with illustrations by Rob Davis and a cover by Ted Hammond.

Pulse-Pounding Pulp Excitement from Airship 27:

PULP MYTHOLOGY
FEATURING
John Henry Vs. the Vampires!

This is just a small sampling of the thrilling tales available from Airship 27 and its award-winning bullpen of the best New Pulp writers and artists. Set in the era in which they were created and in the same non-stop-action style, here are the characters that thrilled a generation in all-new stories alongside new creations cast in the same mold!

"Airship 27...should be remembered for finally closing the gap between pulps and slicks and giving pulp heroes and archetypes the polish they always deserved."
–William Maynard ("The Terror of Fu Manchu.")

Pulp Fiction for a New Generation!

At Amazon.com & www.airship27hangar.com

All Airship 27 Books are available for just *$3/each* at the Airship 27 online hangar! This includes some titles unavailable in print form. For the best in New Pulp reading excitement- *airship27hangar.com!*

www.ingramcontent.com/pod-product-compliance
Lightning Source LLC
LaVergne TN
LVHW010917110826
845149LV00013B/2395
9781969285103